STANDOFF AT THE RIVER

STANDOFF AT THE RIVER

Wayne D. Overholser

GUNSMOKE

This hardback edition 2009
by BBC Audiobooks Ltd
by arrangement with
Golden West Literary Agency

ISBN 978 1 408 46231 7

British Library Cataloguing in Publication Data available.

Printed and bound in Great Britain by
CPI Antony Rowe, Chippenham and Eastbourne

Part One
THE MEN

Chapter 1

DAWN came slowly in the September sky to the camp of Colonel Forsyth's civilian scouts on the Republican, but not slowly enough for some and not fast enough for others. This intrigued Jedediah Jones, who was always interested in the human equation. In a way it separated the eager heroes from the reluctant ones.

Everyone in the command—forty-nine men, two Army officers, and one surgeon—was aware that this was the day when the column would probably catch up with the Indians it had been pursuing. The men were aware, too, that when it happened, many of them, perhaps all of them, would die. Forsyth, or so it seemed to Jedediah, was the only one who did not realize that.

They were on the march up the Republican by the time the first red arc of the sun appeared above the eastern horizon, a long column riding by twos, with Colonel Forsyth and Lieutenant Fred Beecher, the second in command, in front. The guide, Sharp Grover, was always among the flankers out in front or to one side. Jedediah rode halfway back, beside Jamey Burns. Braggin' Bill Harney was opposite Deacon Andy Crowell, and directly ahead of Jedediah.

The scouts followed the river for a time. Then, because the Indian trail led that way, they turned off to go up a dry fork, a trickle of water meandering along its sandy bottom. Dust hung above the command, from Forsyth and Beecher all the way back along the line of march. The climbing plains sun laid a golden glow upon it; it powdered men and horses; it got into the men's noses and ears and mouths and made a nerve-racking, gritting sound between their teeth.

This was not the way it had been when they'd left Fort Hays nineteen days ago. Laughter had been in the men then, and a good deal of horseplay, with young Jamey Burns the butt of their jokes. Their cook fires had been red eyes in the darkness, the prairie spread all around them like a rolling

3

carpet, and the talk had been big and tough about how they'd kill the red bastards that had swept across the Solomon and Saline valleys murdering men, women, and children.

Braggin' Bill Harney's voice had been one of the loudest, but that was before they struck the wide trail they were following this morning, before the feeling was in them that the Indians were just out of sight along the ridges, before fear had spread among them like a destroying, contagious disease. Today there was no laughter.

Harney turned his head to look at Jedediah, his red-rimmed eyes showing the anger that had been growing in him for two days. He demanded: "You know what that God-damned fool Forsyth is doing?"

"Sure I know," Jedediah said.

"I doubt it," Harney snapped. "He's takin' us to a killin'. *Our* killin'. If you knowed that, you wouldn't be here. You'd of left with me last night like I wanted you to."

"Is life that important?" Jedediah asked.

"You're damned right it is," Harney answered. "What else has a man got but his life?"

"His eternal soul," Deacon Andy Crowell said earnestly. "Unless you confess the name of Jesus before you die, you'll be condemned to eternal damnation. You ought to be thinking about that at a time like this."

"What about it, Jed?" Harney demanded, ignoring Crowell as everyone did. "Ain't I right? What else have we got but our lives?"

"Honor."

Jedediah mocked himself with a smile as he considered the word "honor." He had learned long ago that the way to avoid being hurt was not to get involved in anything that had emotional undertones. But here he was using a word that was stamped with emotional undertones, the very thing he tried to avoid as a matter of principle.

Still, there were some things a man could not do, principle or no principle. He added, still smiling, "Aristotle once said, 'It is the nature of many to be amenable to fear, but not to the sense of honor.' "

"Aristotle?" Harney asked. "Is he in the outfit?"

"No," Jedediah answered gravely. "He died some time ago."

Then Harney seemed to catch the significance of the quotation, and he demanded, "You sayin' I'm scared?"

4

"That's the general idea," Jedediah said. "I am. Aren't you?"

"Hell, no," Harney said. "I've just got more savvy than that chowder-headed Forsyth. That's all."

Matthew Redig swung around and gave Harney a look, then turned his head without saying a word. Jedediah did not know exactly what the look meant, for he had never been able to read anything in Matthew Redig's face except that he did not approve of Harney or his talk.

At mid-morning the flankers came in and Forsyth signaled for the command to halt and dismount. With Beecher and Bill McCall, the acting post sergeant, he studied the trail as the guide, Sharp Grover, kept pointing to the west and arguing vehemently about something.

Jamey Burns, standing close to Jedediah, whispered, "Is Harney right, Mr. Jones? Have we got to desert to save our lives?"

"No," Jedediah said. "Your life wouldn't be worth saving if you did."

Jamey looked away and was silent. He kept biting his lower lip nervously and stroking his mustache, his gaze on the men who were conferring at the front of the column. Jedediah knew him better than anyone else in the command, for Jamey had gone to school to him last winter.

Jamey was eighteen, six feet tall and strong, but still a boy. In years he was older than Jack Stillwell, who was one of the flankers up there in front with Forsyth, but Stillwell was already a skilled plainsman. The difference was not one of age. Something was wrong inside Jamey, and Jedediah doubted that any number of years would cure it.

Forsyth gave the order to mount and they rode on, Jedediah glancing at Jamey's pale, tightly drawn face. He had done everything for the kid except blow his nose, from the time they had left Fort Hays. He reflected upon his own inconsistency. In spite of himself, he had become involved with Jamey. The boy was like a pup that had somehow fallen in with a pack of wolves. Jedediah, pitying him, had done what he could, all the time knowing it would not be enough.

They went on till noon, still following the dry fork of the Republican, the flankers out in front and on the sides again. The sun rose steadily into a sky that was without a cloud except that of the dust which lay behind the men, hugging the earth as it spread and lifted until it was finally dissipated into space.

To Jedediah there was something strange and disturbing about the prairie, the eternal sameness, the complete lack of landmarks. He was now twenty-three. From the time he was fourteen until a year ago he had lived in Colorado. If he survived, he would go back. He had to, for he was lost without mountains. Now he wondered why he had stayed away so long.

Here there was land and sky, and the wind you could not see. Nothing else. Overhead the sky was a great blue bowl, sloping down at the edges toward the land, and there at the edges the land tipped up to meet the sky. In between it seemed to run on and on into infinity, showing a gently undulating surface.

Not a tree was in sight anywhere. It would have helped if there had been. Only buffalo grass and brush, with here and there the raw bank of a wash. No matter how far a man rode in a day, he never escaped the eternal land and sky that gave the illusion of meeting out there somewhere beyond where he was.

When the sun reached the high point of its daily arc, the column stopped for the noon meal, a cold bacon sandwich that had been prepared that morning. Now the men took these from their saddlebags, Braggin' Bill Harney staring at his in contempt. He stuffed his mouth and looked around at the men close to him, Jedediah and Jamey Burns and Deacon Andy Crowell. Matthew Redig stood apart from the others as he always did, chewing steadily, a lonely and silent man whose eyes were fixed on Harney in harsh condemnation.

"Look at that damned Army brass hat," Harney said. "All he's doin' is buckin' for a promotion, and he couldn't get it sittin' at a desk on Sheridan's staff. He ain't got sense enough to figure out that it won't do him no good if he's dead."

"He seems competent," Crowell said mildly.

"Competent, hell!" Harney shouted. "By God, we're seven days out of Fort Wallace and our grub's gone. We'd kill game and live off the country, he says. All right, have you seen anything bigger'n a jack rabbit for the last three days? A buffler or an antelope? No, you ain't and the reason is we're behind the biggest batch of Injuns I ever seen. They've hunted the country clean."

Harney jammed the rest of the sandwich into his mouth,

chomped, and pointed at the ground. "Take this here trail. Looks like a beat-down road. See them travois marks in the dirt? This ain't no war party we're trailin'. It's the whole Cheyenne nation. Hundreds of 'em. Maybe thousands, if they hook up ahead with the Sioux. Be some Arapahoes, too, chances are. What Forsyth don't seem to know is that the Injuns won't fight unless the odds are big on their side. That's why they've been on the run. Now they'll quit runnin' 'cause there's enough of 'em to wipe us out to a man."

"I guess Forsyth knows that," Jedediah said. "He figures our Spencer repeaters and Colt revolvers give us enough fire power to handle them."

"And he knows you can't hit the side of a horse more'n a hundred yards off with one o' them Spencers," Harney said. "I've lived with Injuns. I know how they act and how they do." A big hand swept out toward the ridge line to the north. "I tell you they're out there watchin' us, but we ain't watchin' them. We won't, neither, till it's time for 'em to hit us. Then we'll see 'em all right. Chances are we'll see Roman Nose, too. He's the biggest damned Injun in the world. If he's leadin' 'em, God help us, 'cause we sure won't be helpin' ourselves."

Other men had heard his loud voice and had joined the group. One of them said, "You make sense to me, Bill. I'm with you."

"All right, let's pull out. We'll show Forsyth—"

Without a word Redig lunged at Harney, charging between Jedediah and Jamey Burns and sending them spinning. He lowered his head and butted Harney in the soft part of his belly, the wind going out of Harney in a great "Oof." Utterly helpless, he stood paralyzed, bent over, fighting to draw another breath into his lungs.

Jedediah saw the knife flash in Redig's hand. In another instant he would have buried the steel to the hilt in Harney's stomach, but Jedediah leaped forward in time to grab Redig's right arm.

"Give me a hand!" Jedediah yelled. "Andy! Jamey!"

But Jamey stood rooted there, his mouth springing open, and Crowell was slow. Redig was a short-coupled man with tremendous strength in his arms and shoulders; Jedediah was six feet six inches tall and so long-boned and long-muscled that he seemed taller than he was. Now Redig tried to jerk free. Jedediah was like the end man in a game of crack-the-whip. Redig brought his left fist back and hit

Jedediah in the face, but he failed to dislodge him. Then Crowell had Redig's left arm and, with Jedediah, held him helpless, his hands pinned behind his back.

The sergeant, McCall, came on the run. "What's going on here? We've got enough trouble without you fellows cooking up some of your own. Come on. I want to know what happened."

Harney stared at the ground, still struggling for breath. Finally he managed to mutter, "Nuthin', McCall."

Jedediah said, "Go on, Bill. Tell him. I doubt that anybody's going to change the Colonel's mind, but he ought to know what you're thinking."

But Harney shook his head and repeated, "Nuthin', McCall."

"He was leaving," Jedediah said, "and taking any of the men with him who would go. He said we were getting low on rations and it was certain death—"

"I don't care what he said." McCall drew his revolver and jammed the muzzle into Harney's belly. "You son-of-a-bitch! I ought to shoot you where you stand. After all your talk about being a plainsman and living with the Indians and fighting them to hellangone, you're the first one to talk about pulling out."

"I've just got more savvy than anybody else," Harney said.

"Savvy, you call it?" McCall cursed bitterly. "All right, you give some of that savvy of yours to the Colonel." He holstered his revolver and, striding to his horse, mounted and rode back along the column.

Harney stared at Jedediah, irate. "What'd you have to go and tell him for? Last night I figgered on takin' you with me, but you wouldn't go. I thought you'd keep your mouth shut—"

"I like to see a man stand up for what he believes," Jedediah interrupted, "and not try to weasel out of it the way you were doing." He sighed, realizing that Harney wouldn't have the least understanding of such a point of ethics, then added, "If we split up, none of us will have any chance."

"We need every man to shoot Cheyennes," Redig said, "even a yellow bastard like you."

They were the first words Jedediah had heard Redig say that day.

A moment later Forsyth rode up with McCall and both

men dismounted. Forsyth was a young man who, like Lieutenant Fred Beecher, had served with distinction during the recent war. He had been on Sheridan's staff at Fort Harker, Jedediah had heard, but being unwilling to remain at a desk, has asked permission to take the field. Sheridan, having no opening for him and too few troops to run down and punish the Indians for their depredations along the Solomon and Saline Rivers, gave Forsyth permission to enlist fifty scouts and go after the Indians, assigning Lieutenant Beecher from the Third Infantry as his subordinate.

Now Forsyth stood in front of Harney, very tall and very straight, his scornful eyes stripping the hide from the big man and leaving him naked in front of all of them. He said, "I understand you were leaving, Harney."

"No, sir," Harney said, staring at the ground in front of him. "I was just joshin'."

"He's a liar," Redig said.

"He claims we're following the entire Cheyenne nation, not just a war party," Jedediah said. "They'll likely find some Sioux up ahead and maybe some Arapahoes. He says Roman Nose will probably be leading them, and that the Indians will not attack unless the odds are big in their favor."

"I see," Forsyth said. "Anything else, Harney?"

"No. That's plenty, Colonel."

Forsyth looked around the circle of faces. Jedediah saw that the man who had sided with Harney and was going to ride away with him had disappeared.

"You men knew what was expected of you when you joined up," Forsyth said. "Most of you were in the war on one side or the other." His gaze searched out Jedediah. "How about you, Jones?"

"Colorado Volunteers," Jedediah answered.

"All right then, where do you stand? Do you agree with Harney about the Indians?"

"There seems to be some logic in what Harney says and I thought you ought to hear it," Jedediah said, "but it's not a question of whether I agree or not. You're in command."

Forsyth nodded, pleased. "I've heard the same thing from Sharp Grover, but turning back toward Fort Wallace is not the proper course. In my opinion it would be certain death for all of us. The Indians would be on our tail immediately, chewing off every straggler. We have good guns and plenty of ammunition. There will be a lot of them, but we can

9

whip them." His lips curled as his gaze again swept the circle of dusty, sun-reddened faces; then he asked, "You volunteered to fight Indians, didn't you?"

He turned to his horse and, mounting, rode back to the front of the column. McCall laid his gaze on Harney and used his voice like a whip. "I'll promise you one thing, mister, and don't you forget it. I'll shoot the first son-of-a-bitch in the guts who tries to desert." He swung into the saddle and rode after Forsyth at a gallop.

"You know," Andy Crowell said, "I think he will."

"He sure didn't say nuthin' 'bout what we're gonna eat," Harney grumbled.

A moment later the flankers spread out again, Sharp Grover going on up the creek. Forsyth gave the signal to mount and the column started to move.

Jedediah stared thoughtfully at Harney's broad back. He was made of brag and loud talk, but he knew the country and he knew Indians. Jedediah was sure he had not been convinced. He would try again, and if he did, Deacon Crowell was probably right. McCall would shoot him, just as he had promised.

Chapter 2

At four o'clock the column reached a valley about two miles long, with a ridge some distance to the south and low bluffs on the north. Forsyth conferred with Beecher and Grover, and gave the order to camp for the night. Jedediah considered it a wise decision, for there was good graze on the south side of the stream and the horses were tired.

The animals were hobbled and picketed at the end of their lariats. The chore finished, Jedediah crossed the shallow stream, which was about sixty yards wide at this point and consisted of a series of potholes in the sand. He found himself on an island that was perhaps 150 yards long and less than half as wide. It was covered with tall grass and low brush, and Jedediah noticed that there was only a single tree on the lower end of the island, a small cottonwood. It would be lonely, he thought, and then wondered wryly if trees shared that feeling which seemed common to all mankind.

He pushed through the brush to the further bank of the island and looked across the sandy bottom of the north channel of the creek at the bluffs. The Cheyennes were up there, he thought. It was a terrifying feeling, this thing of being watched but never seeing as much as the tip of a feather or the slightest wisp of smoke which might be a signal fire.

His spine felt as if tiny drops of ice water were dripping down its entire length. He wondered if the same feeling was in Forsyth, and whether it had occurred to him, as Harney had suggested, that a dead brevet colonel would find no satisfaction in being a brigadier general.

When he turned, he saw that Jamey Burns was coming toward him through the grass and brush that covered the island. When the boy reached him, he asked again, "Harney was right, wasn't he, Mr. Jones?"

His face was flushed. He kept fingering his mustache, which was a valiant effort in his reaching toward manhood. From his schoolroom experience of the previous winter, Jedediah knew the boy was a dreamer. Dreaming was good for a man if he had some practical sense to go with it, but Jamey didn't have.

Jedediah wondered if that was Forsyth's failing. They had left Fort Wallace with seven days' rations, and this was the seventh day. The last of the beans would be finished for supper. Only coffee and salt would be left. Or was Forsyth overly ambitious? Jedediah didn't know which was the proper explanation, but he did know the results could be fatal in either case.

"Well, was he?" Jamey asked doggedly.

"It's not a question of who's right," Jedediah answered as they started back for the south bank. "Forsyth's in command. He gives the orders. We take them."

"But if Harney is right," Jamey said, "we ought to get together and tell Forsyth we won't take his orders, and start back for Fort Wallace."

"And have the Cheyennes chewing on our flanks and tail?"

"I forgot that," Jamey said, crestfallen.

Jedediah and Jamey joined Deacon Crowell and Bill Harney, who had beans and coffee going over a fire. Crowell was the only member of the command, besides Jamey, that Jedediah had known previously. He lived in the same Kansas community where Jedediah had taught the previous winter. At first he had been obnoxious in his efforts to save souls, but he had met with such scanty success that now he seldom mentioned it.

When Jedediah squatted at the fire beside Crowell, Harney said from the other side of the flames, "You done a damned bad thing to me, Jed."

Jedediah glanced at Matthew Redig, who sat alone beside the next fire. He asked, "Saving your life was a damned poor thing?"

"No, by God!" Harney said angrily. "You know I didn't mean that. I meant tellin' McCall what I said."

"Maybe it needed to be said to Forsyth, if you were right," Jedediah said, and shrugged. "You going to be able to sleep tonight, Bill?"

"Sure. Can't you?"

"I won't even try," Jedediah said. "A man should be alive and conscious and aware of everything he can be during his last hours on earth."

"Then you know I was right," Harney said triumphantly. "Why didn't you tell Forsyth?"

"Running from death is never the answer." The tiny trickle of ice water was dripping down his spine again. "Forsyth gives the orders. If I have to be shot, I'd rather get it from the Cheyennes than from McCall or Forsyth." He glanced at the motionless Redig again. "Or from him."

"I'll slit his throat," Harney said. "By God, I'll cut it all the way down to his belly button."

"The grub's ready," Crowell said.

The sun fell behind the western horizon as they ate; a wild banner of color briefly flared above the western rim of land, then died, and twilight flowed across the valley. Forsyth gave a final order. If they were attacked, every man was to run to his horse and grab the lariat and stand there with his rifle in his hand until he was told what to do.

Double guards were posted, Harney grumbling that it was a fool thing to do. Indians seldom attacked at night, but Forsyth had sure better watch out, come morning. Jedediah wondered if the thought had occurred to Harney that Forsyth was thinking more of losing part of his command than he was of an Indian attack.

Full darkness settled down upon the valley, and most of the men, worn out by a week of hard riding, rolled up in their blankets and went to sleep, Harney and Jamey not far from the fire. Jedediah heard the murmur of talk farther down the creek, and he wished he knew the thoughts that were in the minds of the men before they dropped off to sleep. They had varied reasons for joining the scouts. Revenge. The hunger for adventure. The dollar a day, plus thirty-five cents if they furnished their own horses. But regardless of the reason, Jedediah doubted that any had foreseen the position they were all in tonight.

Matthew Redig let his fire go out and moved to where Jedediah sat. He asked, "All right if I stay here?"

"Sure. Aren't you going to sleep?"

"No," Redig said, and looked past Jedediah at Harney, who was rolled up in his blanket at the fringe of the firelight.

Redig was never one to talk, and now Jedediah didn't want to, either. At a time like this his thoughts ran wild and free and unchanneled. He had only a few hours left for thinking. It was fortunate, he decided, that no man was given the hour when he must die. Knowing would take the fun out of living. Actually, he had never thought much about dying, for at twenty-three it seemed remote. Thinking about death was for old men in their fifties and sixties, but tonight it was not remote for any of them, regardless of the years that lay behind.

He rubbed his hands briskly over the fire, for the night had turned cold as soon as the sun had gone down. He glanced at Redig, sitting on the other side of the fire, dour and silent as usual. He had probably come here to keep Harney from deserting, Jedediah thought. It was a good bet that if Harney tried it, Redig would stop him or kill him.

The night seemed darker than usual, as if a heavy blanket had been spread over the valley with a few tiny holes that were the stars. He heard nothing except the natural and expected sounds: Redig's heavy breathing from the other side of the fire, the stomping of horses along the picket line, the cry of a night bird down the creek, and now and then the lonely call of a coyote from the ridge to the south. But nothing at all from the northern bluffs, and that proved what he already knew, that the Indians were there.

He shrugged his shoulders, telling himself that tomorrow was time enough to be scared, and reaching into his coat pocket, he took out his diary and a stubby pencil. He smiled, wondering why he bothered. The chances were that neither he nor anyone else would be reading it years from now. But he had kept some sort of diary from the time he was twelve; it was a well-established habit, and the truth was he

13

enjoyed putting down his daily entries. He had not missed a night from the day they had left Fort Hays.

The book was well bound with a double leather cover, four by six inches, a convenient size that slipped easily into his pocket. Before he joined the scouts he had kept his journals in various kinds of books, whatever he could find or had on hand, but he had bought this one in Hays City for this particular expedition, knowing they would be out in all kinds of weather. When the outside flap was slipped into the slot prepared for it, the pages were protected against the summer storms that had soaked him more than once since they had ridden out of Fort Hays.

Jedediah opened the book, then closed it, realizing as he thought back over the day's activity that Redig's attack on Harney was unprovoked. Harney was a big wind out of the west, but he was capable enough, and he had never, as far as Jedediah knew, done anything to offend Redig. Then he had the answer. He should have thought of it at once. There had been nothing personal in the attack. Redig simply could not bear the thought of losing a single rifle that would kill Cheyennes tomorrow.

He glanced across the fire again at Redig, who was staring at the flames and apparently not seeing them at all, his broad, Teutonic face stolid and expressionless as it had been from the first day Jedediah had met him at Fort Hays. Leaning forward so he could catch as much of the firelight as possible, Jedediah opened the book to the first blank page and began to write.

On the Dry Fork of the Republican, Sept. 16, 1868

We have found them, or they have found us, whichever way we want to say it. Only God knows how many of them there are, but judging from the wide trail we followed today, there must be hundreds of them. Will Forsyth in his supreme confidence order us to attack them in the morning, or will he wait to be attacked? That, too, is something only God knows, for I doubt that Forsyth does. Most of us expect to die tomorrow, but of all the men in the column, I believe it makes the least difference to Matthew Redig. He is a queer one, never joining in our horseplay and seldom speaking unless forced to, and then usually in a monosyllabic grunt. I wonder if he had always been that way, or did something happen that made him the

*man who sits across the fire from me, a man in whom the
love of life has died? From the few things he has said, it
seems that the only desire he has in life is to kill Cheyennes.*

Chapter 3

TOMORROW was the day for which Matthew Redig had
lived since August 10. Tomorrow he would kill Cheyennes.
At times his memory was like a foggy morning, the sunlight
filtered out and night shadows clinging to a dark earth. At
other times it was sharp and very clear. On those occasions
he remembered how good life had been with his wife Mary
and his sons, fourteen-year-old Mark and baby Luke. But
one thing never changed, his need to kill Cheyennes.

He glanced across the low-burning fire to Jedediah Jones,
who was writing in a small, leather-bound book. A last message to a sweetheart or a wife, Redig thought. A man was
lucky to have someone to love. For him, Matthew Redig,
there was no one. He closed his eyes and he saw it all
again, everything that had happened on that terrible,
bloody day.

On the morning of August 10, 1868, Matthew Redig had
to deliver a milk cow to a new neighbor who lived downstream on the Saline River. He disliked parting with the cow,
but he needed cash to buy the staples for the winter: sugar,
salt, coffee, shoes for all the family except the baby, and a
heavy coat for Mark, who had sprouted up so much the last
few months that he was nearly as tall as his father, his hands
hanging a good six inches below the sleeves of his old,
threadbare coat.

"Saddle Gray Boy for me," he told Mark, and started
toward the house to get his Henry rifle.

Halfway to the front door he stopped and looked around
at the buildings, the neat yard, the cornfield to the east, and
the grassy slope that slanted gently toward the river. This
was his, 160 acres, or would be his when he proved up on it
in three more years. Sometimes, as now, when he thought
about what had happened in the two years since he had
come here, he was filled with a feeling of good fortune,

15

and, oddly enough, a contrary feeling that it could not last.

Every hope and aspiration that had ever been in his mind and heart had found substance here in this piece of land he had marked out and called his. It was home to him and his wife Mary and Mark and Luke, a home for which he had searched many years. He was not a demonstrative man and was never able to put his feelings into words, but he knew that Mary understood he loved her and the boys with a depth of emotion that could not be expressed in words.

He had been with Sherman in his march to the sea. When the war was over, he had drifted, always searching and never being quite certain what he wanted until he saw the valley of the Saline. He knew at once this was it; he picked his quarter section and built a dugout and sent for his family. He realized, as every homesteader did, that he was betting his time and labor against the land, but he was different from the others who had come to the Saline. Some had already given up, others hung on, knowing they would fail, but Matthew Redig would win. There was never the slightest doubt.

They lived in the dugout one year, Redig breaking a patch of sod and planting a crop. He owned a team, a brown mare and a gray gelding that doubled as a saddle horse, and he had a few cows. Early in the second year he hauled oak lumber from Hays City and built a frame house. Not that the dugout wasn't livable. He simply wanted to show his feeling for his wife, and he knew there was nothing he could do that would please her more than giving her a house.

He was handy with tools and he built well. When the house was finished, it was tight against the weather and would be standing here long after Mark and Luke were married and had made him a grandfather. When that day came, he would sit on the porch with Mary and look out across the valley and watch his sons work.

Good stock. Stout fences. A tight barn. Shade trees in front of the house. Close neighbors. A railroad. A county and a county seat. A courthouse. A church. A school for his boys.

These were his dreams, but he was never an idle dreamer. He dreamed while he was holding to the bucking handles of a breaking plow, while he hoed his corn, while he milked. Sometimes he talked to Mark about his dreams, but usually he kept them locked up in his heart. To him they were more than a dream; they were a blueprint of the future.

He went on into the house and stopped to look at Mary, who was kneading bread on the kitchen table. He tried to put the expectancy of disaster out of his mind, tried only to think that he was the luckiest man in Kansas.

"I'll be back as soon as I can," he said, "but it'll be about dark. Gray Boy ain't much on the gallop."

"We'll be all right, Matthew," Mary said, smiling. "What do you want Mark to do today?"

"He can do anything he wants to. Maybe go down to the timber and get us a turkey."

"He'd like that. You go along now. We'll have the chores done before you get back."

Still he hesitated, having an uneasy feeling that he shouldn't go. He had been too lucky, he thought, coming through the war without a scratch, finding this choice piece of land, having a family like he had. The Bible said something about the rain falling on the just as well as the unjust. He was overdue for at least a shower.

He walked back into the front room and stopped at the crib where the baby was sleeping. Born just a year ago last week. Funny how it had been. He'd wanted more of a family than Mark, but he'd given up hope. Then Mary had got pregnant not long after they'd come here, and now she was pregnant again.

"Must be the Kansas air," Mary had said, laughing.

Maybe it was, he thought as he turned toward the door, the rifle in his hand. If this one was a boy, he'd name him John. He hesitated, the uneasy feeling in him growing until it was almost unbearable. He returned to the kitchen and kissed Mary on the cheek. He had never kissed her except at night when they were in bed, but Mark wasn't in the house to see and the baby was asleep. He walked on past Mary to the back door, embarrassed because Mary was staring at him, startled.

"Why, Matthew," she said, pleased. "I'll remember that all day."

He went on outside to find that Mark had saddled the gelding and was holding him at the corral gate. The milk cow that he was to deliver was grazing between the house and the river.

Redig stepped into the saddle and looked down at the boy. He recalled the day he'd gone off to war, marching straight and proud in his blue uniform, and Mark had run along beside the company, yelling, "Good-bye, Daddy. Kill a lot of Johnny Rebs. Kill 'em dead." Weeks later Mary had written that Mark had gone all over town bragging about how his Daddy was killing Johnny Rebs. Ten more men had enlisted because of Mark's bragging.

Now Mark was almost a man, with a streak of peach fuzz on his upper lip that looked like a streak of dirt that never washed off, and a couple of little pimples at the corners of his mouth, and big hands and feet that gave promise of the size he'd grow into.

"Go get us a turkey," Redig said. "You've got a day of fun coming."

Mark showed his surprise, then grinned. "Sure, I'll get a turkey."

"Watch out for the white coyote," Redig said, half-jokingly, and winked.

It was his pet superstition. He'd never seen a white coyote. Maybe there wasn't any. But he'd never forgotten what an old Pawnee had told him years ago. It was bad medicine to see a white coyote. You wouldn't live long if you did. Maybe it had been just a bad joke. Redig had never been sure.

"I'll keep my eyes peeled," Mark said.

Redig grinned and rode away.

Mark watched his father until he disappeared around a bend in the river. He wondered why his father had mentioned the white coyote. He'd shot several coyotes since he'd been here and none of them had been close to white. As far as he knew, no one had ever seen a white coyote. Even if one existed, why would it be bad luck to see it?

Just the superstition of a crazy old Indian, Mark thought as he walked to the house. Indians were always gabbing about "good medicine" and "bad medicine," and if you waited around for your medicine to be good, the way they did, you'd never get anything done. But it did seem queer that his father would mention it today.

A scary feeling touched his spine. Maybe he'd better not go after the turkey. He was the man of the family with Pa gone, and it was his job to look out for Ma and Luke.

When he went into the house, his mother was ironing and the baby was awake and crying. "Pick Luke up a minute, Mark," his mother said. "I guess all this hot weather has upset him."

Mark picked the baby up and rocked him until he dropped off to sleep. He laid Luke back in the crib and returned to the kitchen.

"Maybe I oughtta stay close to the house today," he said. "Why?"

Mark shifted his feet, embarrassed. "Oh, I dunno."

"You go get that turkey," his mother said. "I've been hankering for one since I don't know when, and with all the work this summer, your Pa just never got around to fetching one in."

Mark took the shotgun off the pegs by the back door. He couldn't tell his mother he was scared. He didn't know what he was scared of, really. A rattlesnake? A wolf? Indians? Maybe that was it. There had been some talk about the Cheyennes being proddy, but no one took any stock in it. The folks in the Saline valley said you could always hear that kind of scare talk if you wanted to stand around and listen to it.

"All right, Ma," Mark said finally, and trudged off toward the river.

His luck was bad. He got a shot at one and missed, and after that he couldn't find any, although he followed the river a long way upstream. He was jumpy, every little noise in the brush giving him a start. He didn't know why he was doing it, but he kept looking across the river at the ridge top to the south, and then back the other way.

Funny, he thought, how a shiver gets lodged in your back and stays there. He didn't often feel that way. He remembered he had the time he'd almost stepped on a rattlesnake. And this spring when a cyclone came ripping across the prairie as if it was Old Scratch himself wrapped up in the funnel.

He might just as well have stayed home for all the good he'd do today. He started back, but not long after he left the river he glanced to the south and saw smoke rising above the ridge. Louie Brimhall's house was there. He was the Redigs' nearest neighbor, a bachelor who lived by himself.

Mark went on, thinking his mother wasn't going to like it because he'd missed the only bird he'd seen. She'd probably fix him something to eat and send him back again. Once her mouth started watering for something, nothing could take its place.

"It's on account of her condition," Mark's father told him, but Mark couldn't see what that had to do with it.

He stopped at the edge of a ravine and scanned the north ridge. Nothing showed. He walked on, dropping down the bank and coming up the other side. Again he glanced to the north and stopped, frozen there. He had caught just a glimpse of a coyote slinking along the crest of the ridge. *A white one!* It had been a long way off, but it was white, sure as shootin'.

He started to run toward the house, his heart pounding so hard he thought it was going to come right up out of his throat. He heard something behind him and looked back. He stopped, paralyzed, his breath sawing in and out of his lungs. A band of Indians was riding out of the brush along the river. Ten or twelve of them, painted and almost naked. Cheyennes, he thought at once. Maybe Sioux, but more likely Cheyennes.

They started toward him, putting their ponies into a run. He whirled and stumbled and fell, and got up and ran again. He tried to yell, but his throat was so dry he couldn't make a sound. He had to warn his mother. Had to. He fell again and this time his gun went off. She'd know. She could bolt the heavy oak doors.

He got up and went on, his feet pounding on the carpet of buffalo grass. If he could only reach the sod shed! He glanced back. They were almost on him. No use to keep running. Even the shed might as well have been a mile away. He stopped and turned to face them.

Two braves were a good three lengths of their horses ahead of the rest. Young, not much older than Mark. Both were bending forward, one with a lance, the other with a war club. Mark grabbed his gun by the barrel and, dodging the thrust of the lance, smashed the Indian across the face, bringing him tumbling off his horse. The second brave who was coming in on the other side swung his war club and Mark went down.

He felt nothing when they took his scalp.

Mary Redig was peeling potatoes in the kitchen when she heard Mark's shotgun. She wondered about it. If he were on the river, he'd be too far away for her to hear the report. He must be on his way home. Maybe he'd shot at a prairie chicken, or a rattlesnake.

She didn't give it another thought until she heard the baby cry. She ran into the front room, then she screamed, an involuntary outcry. The room was crawling with Indians. It stunk with the smell of them.

She started toward the crib when one of the braves said, "Coffee."

She stopped, and her hand came up to her throat. She had coffee on the stove. They loved it with sugar. Maybe if she gave it to them, they wouldn't hurt her and Luke. Mark was dead. She didn't have to be told—it was something she knew.

She ran back into the kitchen and brought tin cups out of the pantry. Her hand was shaking as she lifted the coffee pot from the stove and filled the cups. She didn't have enough for all of them.

"I'll make more," she said, hoping that at least one of them understood English.

She reached for the sugar bowl and spooned some into each cup, her hand shaking so badly that she spilled some on the table. They were almost out of sugar—coffee, too.

As she turned toward the stove, the Indian she had given a cup to spat a mouthful on the floor and yelled in derision. "Tin cup, hell!" he said. "Me mad."

She stopped, staring at the painted face that seemed to her the embodiment of all that was evil. Then she understood. He was insulted because she had served him coffee in a tin cup.

"I have some china cups," she said. "I'll get them."

She saw that one of the Indians had taken Luke from his crib and brought him into the kitchen. She cried out, and ran toward the baby, but one of the Indians hit her and slammed her against the wall. Grinning, the Indian who held Luke took him by the feet and smashed his head against the door casing, blood and brains spilling from his skull.

She dropped to her knees, screaming, "My God! Oh, my God!"

She never saw the descending tomahawk that split her skull.

Matthew Redig did not accept his neighbor's invitation to stay for dinner. He took the money and started back at once, kicking Gray Boy into a trot, but the horse was exasperatingly slow.

Redig seldom left home, and now he wished he hadn't today. He wasn't worried about his family, he told himself. Mary was no hothouse Eastern woman who was terrified of the prairie, and Mark was not a boy who ducked his responsibilities. But he'd be down on the river hunting and Mary would be alone with the baby. Redig wished he hadn't told Mark to go after a turkey.

He left the river which made a bend to the south, and angled across a ridge, a short cut that saved him a quarter of a mile. He smelled the smoke first, then glimpsed a faint haze to the west. He wouldn't be able to see what it was until he reached the top of the ridge, and he began to worry. He was getting back earlier than he had expected, but still it was the tag end of the afternoon, his and Gray Boy's shadow a long, grotesque shape following him on the buffalo grass.

He was a long way from home when he reached the crest of the ridge, but he could see what was left of his house, and he flogged Gray Boy into a laboring run. He prayed that this wasn't what he was afraid it was. He had heard the talk about the Indians being restless, but none of the settlers on the Saline had thought it was anything more than talk. They had worried when the Cheyennes had made a raid on the Kaws at Council Grove, but that had been in June, and Redig hadn't heard of any more trouble.

The sun was almost down when he reached the smoldering ashes, all that was left of the house. Mary's and the baby's bodies were in the yard. He walked toward them, slowly, unable to think or to feel, an automaton with the power of locomotion.

He circled the smoking pile of ashes, then walked in that same slow manner around the sod shed and found Mark's body. He went back to Mary and stared at her bloody, battered head, then he sat down and, putting his arms around her body, lifted her to his lap and held her close. He sat there rocking back and forth.

He was still there the next morning when a neighbor came by. The man had to fight an almost overpowering sickness that rose in him when he saw the bodies. Finally, when he could speak, he put a hand on Redig's shoulder and said, "I'm sorry, Matthew. Damned sorry."

Redig looked at him as if he did not see him. The neighbor said, "Louis Brimhall is dead." Still Redig was silent. Then the man said, "We'll have to bury your people. Can't let it go in this heat. We couldn't get them to Hays City."

The neighbor waited until he realized there was nothing he could do or say that would reach Redig. He went to the shed and, finding a spade, dug three shallow graves. He put Mark in one, the baby in another, and then he had a hard time struggling with Redig before he could loosen the big arms which were wrapped tightly around Mary's body. When he finally succeeded, he left Redig sitting there, his head tipped forward so that his chin rested against his blood-smeared shirt.

The man filled the graves, put a rope around the neck of the mare that was in the corral, and returned to Matthew. He said, "We've got to ride. You ain't got nothin' to stay here for now."

But Redig didn't hear and he didn't move. The man slipped his hands under Matthew's armpits and lifted him to his feet. He stood there, swaying, his gaze on the eastern horizon.

"You've got to walk, Matthew," the man said. "Walk to your horse."

Redig obeyed, his head lifted, his eyes wide and unblinking. Somehow the man got him into the saddle and put the reins in his hands. He mounted his own horse and, leading the mare, rode slowly down the river. Matthew followed, his head high, his eyes fixed on some far point that was not visible to the man riding beside him.

Chapter 4

JEDEDIAH closed his book and glanced up at the stars. Getting on toward midnight, he thought. Behind him Harney began to snore with long, gurgling sounds. Jedediah reached out to prod him into wakefulness, then dropped his hand. Harney might as well enjoy himself. No harm could come from his snoring.

Jedediah turned back to the fire, aware that Lieutenant Beecher had appeared out of the darkness and squatted beside him. Beecher said, "A cold night for this time of year."

"Too cold," Jedediah said.

Beecher glanced at him curiously. "Can't you sleep, Jones?"

"Why should a man waste the last hours of his life sleeping?" Jedediah asked.

"Oh, come now," Beecher said impatiently. "You haven't exactly been condemned to death."

"Every man is condemned to death the day he is born," Jedediah said. He was silent a moment, then added, "The questions are when and how and where, and how many debts a man leaves behind him. The only person I owe anything to is a girl. I'd give you a message to take to her, but it would be a waste of time. If I'm not alive to tell her, the chances are you won't be, either."

Beecher stared at the fire, his expression a thoughtful one. Finally he said, "During the war I knew of men who seemed to have premonitions of death. They wrote letters to their loved ones and gave them to friends to mail when the battle was over. It's my opinion that we hear about the cases in which the premonitions turned out the way the soldiers expected. On the other hand, I suspect that there were hundreds of cases in which the men lived through the fighting, but perhaps their friends who had the letters were killed."

"I don't have any premonition," Jedediah said. "I was with the Colorado Volunteers at the battle of Glorieta in New Mexico. I didn't think about dying any more than the next man, because the odds were about even; but what are the odds we'll be bucking tomorrow?"

Beecher smiled. "A conservative guess would be about ten to one. If you're a gambling man, you figure the odds; but if you're a soldier, you fight and do your best to kill the enemy and stay alive. You're a soldier, Jones, not a gambling man."

He nodded, still smiling, and rose. Jedediah watched him as he walked along the line of sleeping men and disappeared into the darkness, limping because of a leg wound which he had received at the battle of Gettysburg and which had never properly healed. Here was a man who had earned the right to be called a soldier, Jedediah thought.

Quite likely Beecher had his reservations about Forsyth's ability in this kind of campaign, Jedediah told himself. The Colonel had never fought Indians and did not understand them. Beecher did, so he must have questioned Forsyth's wisdom in pursuing such a large party so far from Fort Wallace with rations running low, but he would not criticize his commanding officer.

Beecher was here because he was ordered to be here. Jedediah was here because he had made the decision to join Forsyth's scouts, not because of an order Phil Sheridan had given.

Having been cursed with an inquiring mind from the time he had been a small boy, Jedediah wondered about the reasons the men had for joining. He glanced at Matthew Redig's face, as unchanging as the face of the prairie itself. Perhaps the man sought death. If he did, probably he would find it, but this was not the case with Jedediah.

He knew why he was here, but he was not proud of the reason. He was never proud of running from something, even a girl. He was ashamed, and being ashamed, he opened his book and began to write, finding some strange satisfaction in indicting and condemning himself of stupidity.

Chapter 5

JEDEDIAH finished writing and, holding the book toward the fire, read what he had just written.

If I could see Cally now, I would tell her I loved her. I would marry her tonight if I could. I would make her pregnant as often as I could and we would raise as many children as we could. I would be proud of her and of them. Because I am a free man with a free will to make decisions, I made the wrong one. If a man cannot accept the love a woman offers him, and if he refuses to recognize his love for her, he deserves the destiny he has brought upon himself and he deserves the sympathy of no man.

Jedediah closed the book and slipped it into his coat. Staring at the fire, he remembered how it had been, that last evening with Cally Moore.

Jedediah always hated to see a period of his life come to an end, especially when the period had been a pleasant one. Both his teaching and his boarding with old Mike Fernoy had been pleasant, and now, having finished supper, he realized with regret that this was the end. It was the evening of August 27, 1868. In the morning he was riding to Fort Hays to join Colonel George Forsyth's scouts.

Taking a cigar from his pocket, he lighted it and drew on it with relish. He said, "You know, Mike, when I took the Laura's Tit school last fall, folks said I was crazy to board with an old coot of a bachelor like you, but I've never regretted it. You're a good cook."

"Thank you kindly," Fernoy said. "Now are you going to see Cally?"

Jedediah shook his head. "Looks to me as if we'd both be better off if I ride out in the morning and give Cally a chance to forget me."

Fernoy's knotted fist slammed against the table, making the dishes rattle. "You've got more book larnin' than anybody I know, but by grab, you're either mean or stupid. I'd be ashamed to treat a heifer calf the way you treat Cally."

"I'm not mean, Mike. Let's say I'm stupid."

"All right, you're stupid. Still leavin' in the mornin'?"

"Before sunup," Jedediah said. "Sheridan ordered Forsyth to enlist fifty scouts. If I'm not among the first fifty, I'll get left out."

"You'd be a damned sight better off if you did get left out," Fernoy grumbled. "You know as much about scoutin' as you know about women."

"More," Jedediah said. "No man knows anything about women."

"You're comin' back when the scrap's over, ain't you?"

Jedediah shook his head. "No, there's a lot of country I haven't seen. I'm a drifter, Mike. I didn't aim to stay here, but they needed a teacher and I needed a job, so I stayed. Now it's time to travel."

"You just want to get away from Cally," Fernoy said hotly. "She's in love with you, and you know it. What you don't seem to know is that you're in love with her, and that makes you purty dad-burned stupid."

Jedediah took the cigar out of his mouth and inspected the ash. "I've pleaded guilty to that already."

"You're stupid on another count," Fernoy said. "You shouldn't of resigned your job. Folks like you. Even the kids. Why, just the other day Jamey Burns told me he was sorry you wasn't teachin' next year. Claimed you was the best teacher he ever had, and him a man grown. Hadn't even been in school for two years till you came along."

There was too much truth in what Fernoy was saying for Jedediah to sit here and listen to more of it. He rose. "All right, I'll go over and see Cally if it will get you off my neck."

"Might pleasure you some," Fernoy said.

"Might be downright painful, too," Jedediah said.

He went out through the back door, ducking as he did from long habit. He was tall enough to get his head cracked in a good many doorways if he didn't stoop when he went through them.

People fastened a variety of nicknames on him, such as

Highpockets, Needles, Slim, and others that he liked less, but almost anything was preferable to being called Jedediah, the name his father, Nehemiah Jones, had fastened upon him. He had never heard what his paternal grandfather's name was, but it had likely been Obadiah, Zephaniah, or Malachi.

He tossed his cigar into the bare dirt of the yard, wishing he hadn't thought of his father. He never did consciously, but thoughts were insidious things which had a way of slipping into the mind unbidden. He had many boyhood memories that were painful, but none as painful as those of his father, who had raised him from infancy, his mother having died when he was a baby.

Oh, he owed a great deal to his father—he was honest enough to admit that. Fourteen years of care and love. His affection for books. A code of morals. But there was the other side of it which he did not understand at all, not even after nine years of thinking about it. He had loved and trusted his father as he had never loved or trusted another human being, but it had meant nothing to Nehemiah Jones, who had simply gone off and left him.

Necessity had taught him long ago to accept the realities of life, to take what came and make the most of it, and he was inordinately proud of the fact that he had earned his living for the last nine years.

Reddy, his sorrel horse, trotted to the corral gate when he whistled. He patted the animal's neck as the horse nuzzled him, then he saddled up. He mounted and rode across the prairie to Cally Moore's house, skirting the bowl-like elevation known locally as Laura's Tit.

The story was that an early settler had a wife who possessed remarkable physical adornments. She was the cause of a fight between her husband and a neighbor, the husband killed the neighbor and got his neck stretched, and Laura promptly left the country. Although the women of the community considered Laura's Tit an inelegant name, they had not succeeded in changing it.

The story illustrated one of Jedediah's basic beliefs, that a man was foolish to get emotionally involved in anything. If the husband hadn't been in love with Laura, he wouldn't have killed the neighbor, he wouldn't have had his neck stretched, and in all likelihood he would be alive today.

The sorrel hadn't been ridden all day and he wanted to go, so Jedediah let him out. He didn't pull the animal up until he reached Cally's house, and all the time he was riding he asked himself what he could say to the girl.

He wasn't responsible for her loving him. Oh, he'd taken Cally to dances and basket socials and the meetings of the literary society at the schoolhouse, and even to Deacon Andy Crowell's church. He had kissed her and enjoyed it, but not in the way she had. He just couldn't forget where it would take him if he wasn't careful. The truth was, Cally wanted a husband, but he didn't want a wife.

Cally had a lot in her favor, though, and that bothered him. She understood what he said, which no one else in the district did when he started one of his lengthy discourses, and she could quote as many poets and philosophers as he could. She was a good cook. And she was pretty.

These assets added up to making Cally an ideal wife, but, as Shakespeare said, that was the rub. A wife was the last thing he wanted, for marriage was a state of emotional involvement to the full.

The instant he dismounted in front of the Moore house, Cally bounced out of the house and came on across the yard, calling, "I thought you had forgotten where I live, Mr. Jones."

"Well, I didn't," he said.

She was, as Mike Fernoy expressed it, as pretty as a bay filly. Just an even five feet, with sharp blue eyes and hair as gold as a patch of wheat ready for the threshing. With both hands she took hold of his vest that was unbottoned and held up her lips. When he hesitated, she said, "Don't keep a lady waiting when she wants to be kissed."

He obliged, then she danced away, taking his hand and leading him toward the walnut grove by the creek. He went reluctantly, wishing he could just say good-bye and ride back to Fernoy's place. But he owed her more than that, he guessed, this being the last time he'd ever see her.

Cally dropped to the ground as soon as they reached the grove. They were out of sight of the house here, although Jedediah judged that was not a pertinent point. Cally was an old maid by the local standards, so her folks would stay out of the way and let her use any strategy she needed to trap a husband.

They sat in silence for a time, the hot August twilight becoming night. A cricket began a cheerful concert from somewhere in the deep grass near the creek, and a long-winged bird zoomed out of the sky overhead and turned sharply and disappeared.

Finally Cally said, "I just heard you aren't going to teach next year."

28

"No." He hesitated, then decided he might just as well get it over with. "I'm leaving early in the morning to join a column of scouts that Colonel Forsyth is taking west to fight Indians. They've got to be punished for what they did on the Saline and the Solomon."

He heard her shocked gasp; then she said in a low voice, "You might not come back."

He pretended he didn't know what she meant. "I don't intend to. I'm just a tumbleweed. I've been here almost a year. That's long enough."

"Why are you doing this? You don't really care about punishing the Indians, do you?"

"Oh, not particularly, but it will be an experience."

"You aren't telling me the real reason you're going," she said stubbornly. "I want to hear this beautiful theory of yours about how to be happy. I want to pick holes in it."

"You can't, but I'll let you try," he said. "It's like this. Every human being is selfish. People spend their lives searching for happiness, but they search in the wrong way because they get involved with people or causes or something, so they end up disappointed and unhappy. You think about the people you know. Can you name one who is happy? Except me, of course."

"I know one thing," she said sharply. "You're not happy."

"Sure I am. I don't get involved, so I'm never disappointed, and therefore I'm happy."

"Oh, rot!" She reached out and put a hand on his arm. "You must have been terribly hurt at one time or you wouldn't have such crazy notions. And they *are* crazy, Jedediah. You're smart enough to know that real happiness comes from being involved, from loving and planning and seeing those plans succeed."

"All right, Cally," he said cheerfully, "you believe what you want to. But I'm surprised that you're taken in by the same illusion that traps so many people."

She sighed. "Jedediah, you're a great one to quote famous writers to prove your point. Well, I can do some quoting too. I was reading John Donne the other day and I found a paragraph I liked. It goes like this: 'No man is an island, entire of itself; everyone is a piece of the continent, a part of the main. If a clod be washed away by the sea, Europe is the less, as well as if a promontory were, as well as if a manor of thy friend's or of thine were. Any man's death diminishes me, because I am involved in mankind, and therefore never send to know for whom the bell tolls; it tolls for thee.' "

He knew the passage. Suddenly he realized with keen regret that he would miss Cally. She was a stimulus, a challenge, a hone upon which he had sharpened his mind many times in the months he had known her. She deserved something better than a plodding farmer whose vision did not extend past his quarter section of land, but that was probably the kind of man she would marry.

"I guess you don't have anything to say to that," she prodded after a moment of silence.

"Only one thing I can say. Even John Donne was taken in by the same illusion you are."

"Oh, that's not worthy of you," she said angrily. "Jedediah, you can't go. You just can't."

"I certainly can. Every American is a free man who has the inalienable right to—"

"That's not what I mean, and you know it. I love you. You must know that, just as I know you love me, but you would die before you'd tell me or even admit it to yourself."

"Love is the greatest illusion of all," he said. "Well, I've got to go. I just came over to say good-bye."

"Jedediah, is there anything in this world you love except your horse?"

"No, I guess not," he said. "There's a big difference between a human and a horse, you know. You can always count on the horse."

She was lying on her side, looking at him, her face an expressionless oval in the darkness. She whispered, "Would— would you kiss me good-bye?"

"Why, it would be a pleasure," he said.

She didn't come to him, or even sit up, so he lowered his face to hers, an arm going around her. Instantly her hands came up and gripped him and pulled him down beside her, and she was an electric storm in his embrace, her hungry mouth on his. He was a man caught in a rushing current and being carried toward the falls. He tried to push her away, but it shocked him to find that he was only trying half-heartedly.

"I love you so much," she whispered. "I want you to be the father of my children. You can't go, Jedediah. You can't leave me."

Her words broke the spell. He took her by the shoulders and frantically shoved her away from him and got up and

30

ran toward his horse in leggy, hurried strides. He swung into the saddle and galloped away. Later he pulled the horse down. Sweat covered his face. He wiped a sleeve across his forehead. It was a long time before his heart gentled down and stopped the wild pounding.

When he reached the Fernoy place, old Mike was waiting up for him. He asked truculently, "Still leaving?"

"You bet I am," Jedediah answered.

"You're a damned fool if I ever seen one," Fernoy said in disgust. "You ain't one to learn from another man's experience, but I'll tell you mine anyway. Folks think I'm teched, livin' alone this way, and mebbe I am, but there's a reason. I was in love once, but I was like you—never knowed it. Couldn't be tied down by no woman and kids, I says to myself, so I went and left her, but one day I figgered out I'd made a mistake. I went back, but she hadn't waited on me."

"All right, Mike," Jedediah said. "I've heard your sermon. Now I'm going to bed."

He went into his room and closed the door. He took off his clothes and lay down on the bed, but he couldn't sleep. He could see Cally's face in the darkness as clearly as if she were here in the room with him and it was daylight. He wished it was dawn and he could be on his way to Fort Hays and then maybe she would go away and let him alone.

Chapter 6

JEDEDIAH rose from where he had been sitting by the fire and stretched. He had been sitting there a long time. Matthew Redig had not moved. Probably he would remain exactly as he was until dawn and Forsyth gave an order, or the Indians attacked. It was a question in Jedediah's mind which would come first.

He walked away from the fire into the quiet darkness toward the picket line, smelling the horse nitrogen that was not unpleasant to him. Suddenly an animal squealed in anger and kicked at his neighbor, then there was silence again. A sentry challenged Jedediah, he identified himself, and went on.

He stopped and stared at the sky. Past midnight now. He asked himself why he had ridden half the length of Kansas, northwest almost to the Nebraska line, angled southwest with the column to Fort Wallace, and finally northwest again to this camp on the Dry Fork of the Republican, all for the grim purpose of dying. Then he wondered why he let the question ride him the way it did. Certainly there was no part of wisdom in the answer.

Cally had not left his mind as he had hoped she would after he had joined the scouts. She had been beside him by day and she had slept with him at night, and she had whispered over and over in his ear, "I love you so much." He tried to find comfort in the thought that he had done what was best for her. She would forget him in time.

If he had married her, he could not have spent the rest of his life teaching the Laura's Tit school or helping old Mike Fernoy farm. No, he'd soon have been on the move again, taking her with him, making her face the same privations he did, perhaps even going into Indian country where she would suffer the same fears and possibly the terrible death that so many settlers' wives on the Saline and the Solomon had suffered only last month.

This was better. Sure, she would forget him in time and marry a farmer and raise her family. She would be happy, as happy as anyone who believed in the great illusion could be. And yet, after telling himself this over and over, he never quite convinced himself.

He returned to the fire, cursing himself under his breath. He could not, even now, turn his back upon the principle that had guided him through the years after his father had left him. Not overnight, anyhow. Maybe he never could— he wasn't sure.

He did know that if he exposed himself again to love, he exposed himself to pain, and he could not stand it again. Not after it had taken him so long to get over the heartache that had followed his father's desertion. No, he had lived the only way he could, keeping himself aloof from anything that meant emotional involvement.

When he reached the fire, he found Jamey Burns beside it. The boy looked up and tried to smile, but his lips were too frozen to obey. He said, "I couldn't sleep, Mr. Jones."

Jedediah would be "Mr. Jones" to him as long as they were together. He thought derisively that his principle wasn't such a guiding one after all, not after looking out for Jamey from the time they had left Fort Hays, and after interfering in the fight between Billy Harney and Matthew Redig.

He would not soon forget the afternoon they had left the fort, August 29, a cold and drizzly day. Jamey had done everything wrong. His equipment—carbine, revolver, roll of blankets, saddlebag, all of it—refused to stay in place. He was constantly shoving something back to where it should be, then it started shifting again. He was chafed by the saddle and, being wet from the rain, the belts that were supposed to keep his equipment where it belonged made his skin red and tender.

Unfortunately, his horse was a fast walker and repeatedly worked ahead of his place in line. Jamey, of course, was ordered back into place. The result was that his bridle hand became so sore and stiff it was almost useless.

That night he was too tired to eat his supper. The final irony was the fact that he was detailed for guard duty, and when Jedediah relieved him, he was asleep. At another time and under different circumstances, he would have been shot, but Jedediah wasn't sure the boy fully understood that even yet.

From that first day Jamey was the butt of every joke the men could think of. Jedediah had comforted him, advised him, tried to give him courage, and all the time had known that no one could help Jamey Burns through the trial by fire that waited for all of them.

Jedediah squatted beside Jamey now and lighted a cigar. He said, "I can't either, Jamey. Are you scared?"

"You know I am." Jamey turned his face to Jedediah. "I'm more scared than I ever was in all my life."

Jedediah thought of several things he could say. If he were Forsyth or Beecher, he would probably have said they would fight tomorrow, and if they must die, they would die like men. But talk like that wouldn't do Jamey any good.

He put a hand on the boy's shoulder. "We're all scared, Jamey. Most of us are honest enough to admit it. Now you go on back and try to get some sleep. We're going to have to shoot straight in the morning."

Jamey said, "All right, Mr. Jones," and rose and disappeared into the darkness.

Jedediah reached toward his pocket for his diary, then his hand dropped away. He had nothing to write about Jamey Burns except two questions. Why had he enlisted in the scouts? Why had Forsyth taken him? But unanswered questions never decided anything. They weren't worth the space they would take.

Chapter 7

JAMEY couldn't sleep. He wished he could, but all he could do was to lie here in his blankets and shiver. Not from the cold, although it was cold enough. He would be shivering if the night was hot. He was scared. That was the God-awful truth, scared so thoroughly and completely that he was frozen inside. Even the night noises that were perfectly normal seemed inordinately loud because they might mean the presence of Indians.

He had always lived in a land of make-believe; he had seen himself as a great hero saving battle after battle by his courage, but he had never considered the other side of it, the privations and the weariness and the physical danger. Life at home hadn't been easy, but it hadn't been hard either, not really hard. Now that it was too late, he understood that, but he should have understood it all the time. All he could do now was to ask himself why he had been such a fool.

Jamey Burns hated weeds. He hated corn almost as much. He hoed down a row, letting the blade fall of its own weight in hopes it would cut off a weed. This was August 27. Cold weather would come soon and the weeds would stop growing.

He guessed he hated weeds more than corn. Nobody made any money out of weeds, but if Pa was lucky, he'd make a few dollars out of the corn. Not that it would do Jamey any good. Or Ma, either, unless she was on hand to grab the money out of Pa's fist. If she didn't, he'd ride into Hays City and get roaring drunk. Then Jamey would have to do the milking until Pa sobered up and got over the fantods and they let him out of the jug.

Pa had been a hard drinker as long as Jamey could remember. They'd moved here from eastern Kansas after the

34

war, Pa claiming they'd get away from the chills and fever. Well, they had done that, but they weren't any better off than they had been, and Pa kept right on drinking.

The way Jamey saw it, Pa had only one thing to his credit: his service in the Sixth Kansas Cavalry during the war. According to him, he'd given a pretty good account of himself. Jamey had a notion his tales were true, judging from the fights he got into around Ellsworth.

A salty outfit, that Sixth Kansas Cavalry. Only half of them had worn uniforms. According to Pa, they hadn't needed a commissary train. They'd just lived off the country, having no conscience about what they took. Maybe that was what made them the fighting fools they were. Pa was right prideful about belonging to that regiment, and Jamey allowed that for once maybe he had a right to be.

Life hadn't been fair to Jamey. He'd been only fifteen when Lee surrendered, but he'd been big for his age. He could have been a drummer boy, all right, but Ma said no, he had to stay home. She couldn't do without him. The truth was she didn't want him to get hurt.

Ma spoiled him, and that was a fact. Pa was always telling her so. He was wrong on almost everything, but he was right on that. Ma saw him as a little boy and he guessed she always would. Like calling him Jamey. He wanted to be called Jim. That was a man's name, but no, Ma called him Jamey, so everybody else did, too. Even the teacher, Jedediah Jones.

That was another case where Pa was wrong. Jamey hadn't been in school for a while, the Laura's Tit district having women teachers who couldn't keep order. Then they hired Mr. Jones and Ma said it was time for Jamey to have a little more book learning. Pa bucked it, but Ma won. She usually did. She wasn't any bigger than a cricket, and Pa was one size larger than a Percheron stud horse, but when it came right down to cases, she usually handled him.

It had been fun to see Mr. Jones keep order. The first day the McIver kid started being ornery, so Mr. Jones grabbed him and horsed him into the aisle, then he got him by the seat of the pants and his shirt collar and heaved him through the front door on his face. Mr. Jones said not to come back. The boy didn't, but his dad did.

Old man McIver was big and ornery, and had a reputation for being a mean knife fighter. He rode up on his mule in the middle of the afternoon and stomped into the schoolhouse. Mr. Jones took his knife away from him and hit him twice. That did it. Everybody in the district allowed that he carried considerable authority in either fist.

Quite a man, Mr. Jones was. He was a shark at ciphering, he could spell anybody else down in the district, and he could out-argue anyone except Cally Moore at the debates they had at the literary society meetings.

And reading? Why, nobody could mention a book Mr. Jones didn't know about. Every morning he read aloud for fifteen minutes, "Hiawatha" maybe, or about King Arthur and his Knights of the Round Table. He read so you thought it was happening right there in front of you and you got chills up and down your back and you couldn't even take a good breath.

Pa allowed Jamey didn't learn a thing that did him a mite of good—just made him lazier. The truth was Jamey sneaked some of Mr. Jones's books home and sat up most of the night reading, so he didn't have much energy the next day. Besides, he kept thinking about Lancelot or Merlin or maybe Aladdin instead of the work he was supposed to be doing.

Mr. Jones said a man needed to dream, that all the big things in the world had been done by men who dreamed. Sure, men like Eli Whitney and Robert Fulton worked hard, but if they hadn't dreamed first, their work wouldn't have amounted to anything.

The way Jamey saw it, he'd been born too late. There wouldn't be another war for fifty years, so he wouldn't have a chance to amount to anything. If he had been a little older, he'd have been a general by the time Gettysburg was fought. He'd have won the war a year sooner than Grant had and he'd have marched right down to Richmond and made a prisoner out of old Jeff Davis and . . .

"Jamey," Pa bellowed.

He dropped the hoe handle and whirled. He didn't know Pa had sneaked up on him. Every time he looked at Pa, it seemed to Jamey he got uglier, with that big chin and a black mole at the corner of his mouth and a nose red enough to light a fire with.

"By God, you hoe like an old maid waving good-bye to her lover," Pa bellowed in a voice that could have been heard clean down to the Laura's Tit store. "Half of the weeds you hoed will keep right on growing with all them roots you're leaving in the ground."

Pa stopped to draw a breath, his face purple. Someday he'd

have a stroke, getting so mad. He tried three times to swallow before he finally made it, then he said, "I'm going to town for a load of lumber to build that chicken house your Ma wants, and you'd better have this hoeing finished by the time I get back. You hear?"

"Yeah, I hear," Jamey said.

Pa whirled and stomped off. Jamey worked hard for ten minutes. By that time Pa had rattled off with the wagon. Jamey threw the hoe down. He could work out here in the sun until he was worn down to a nubbin and all the good he'd do would be to raise corn to make money to buy whisky for Pa. To hell with it.

He'd run off. He'd go to Fort Hays and join the Army. They needed soldiers to fight the Indians. By fall he'd be telling General Sheridan what to do. After what had been happening in the Saline and Solomon valleys, he guessed Sheridan needed somebody to tell him what to do.

Jamey owned a mouse-colored gelding and a saddle and the clothes on his back. He'd be all right once he got to Fort Hays. He considered saddling up and leaving right then, but he ought to tell Ma good-bye. And there was Ruth Tilton, who lived on the next farm.

He guessed he was in love with Ruth. It was a lot of fun kissing her and holding hands. She'd been pestering him to marry her ever since school was out, but she was only sixteen and so far he'd been able to put her off. She was kind of homely, but Jamey didn't mind that. She listened to him tell about the things he was going to do and sometimes he read to her and she liked that, especially the poetry.

He'd better see her before he left. He'd be a colonel in a few months. A major anyway, and he'd have a big salary so he could get married. He glanced at the house. Ma wasn't watching, so he struck off toward the Tilton farm.

He had to be careful, because old man Tilton didn't want him to see Ruth. He always hid in a swale below the Tilton house, and if he hooted like an owl for a while, Ruth would show up if she could sneak out.

Funny thing. Ma didn't want him to see Ruth any more than the Tiltons did. She just didn't like them. She said they were goody-goody psalm singers who didn't know their own privy stunk. They belonged to Deacon Crowell's church and thought God looked like Jacob Tilton. He had a long beard, the kind John Brown used to wear. Ma said God didn't look like that at all.

Jamey lay down in the grass when he reached the swale

and hooted a few times and waited. In about ten minutes Ruth walked past him, made a half circle as she looked back at the house, and then ducked down and ran to him. He took her into his arms and kissed her.

"Your mustache tickles," she said, and giggled.

He guessed she liked it all right, because she kept on kissing him. When she finally got tired, he told her he was running away and she began to cry.

"You've got to take me with you," she begged. "I'm tired of being told I've got to be good so I can go to heaven. Deacon Crowell's coming over tonight to pray for me, but I don't want to be good. I want to be with you."

"I'll come back and marry you," he promised. "As soon as I get to Fort Hays they'll give me a white horse and a sword. I'll be on General Sheridan's staff in a few months. As soon as I catch Roman Nose and Dull Knife and Black Kettle, they'll make me a general. I'll have a big salary and I'll fetch you to the fort."

"Jamey, it sounds so good," she whispered.

"I'll fetch you some scalps."

"Scalps?" She shivered in delight. "Isn't that kind of awful?"

"Kind of," he agreed, "but it's what they all do."

Neither of them saw old man Tilton until he stood over them, his arms folded, his black eyes filled with as much fury as Pa's had been an hour before. He said, "Ruth."

She rolled away from Jamey and got up, her face red as she smoothed her dress down. Her father caught her by a shoulder and shook her. "Go fetch me the buggy whip," he ordered. "I've told this young whelp to stay away from here, and now I find him leading you down the road to perdition in broad daylight. I'll make him wish he'd never seen you."

"Pa, he's going to fight Indians."

"Fight Indians?" Tilton roared a laugh, his beard fluttering as if it were caught in a high wind. "He'll fight Indians like his father takes the pledge. Get me that buggy whip."

Ruth trudged toward the barn, Tilton folding his arms again and glaring at Jamey. "By Heaven, if you've made her with child, I'll see that you marry her."

Jamey was as scared as he had ever been in his life. Old man Tilton would lay the buggy whip on with a vengeance. Jamey was on his feet edging away and now he ducked past the old man and started to run, but Tilton grabbed his shoulder. He wiggled and clawed and kicked, and finally broke free.

Jamey ran and didn't look back, but he heard Tilton yell, "If you ever come back here, I'll dust you off with buckshot."

Jamey kept going, over the ridge between the two farms and around the barn. He went right to the corn patch and picked up the hoe. Ma was out looking after the chickens. She saw him and called, "What's the matter, Jamey?"

He hoed like a wild man and pretended he didn't hear. By sundown when Pa got back he wasn't quite done, but Pa took a look and said grudgingly, "That's better. You'd best come in for supper or Ma'll have a fit. You can finish in the morning."

He obeyed. No use to tell Pa he'd be down the road a piece, come morning. When he came back, he'd have that white horse and a sword, and maybe he'd use it to trim old man Tilton's beard.

"Jamey, what are you mumbling about?" Ma asked. "Eat your supper. I fried the chicken just the way you like it."

"Yes, Ma," Jamey said, and bent his head over his plate. He hadn't known he was mumbling.

When Jamey finished eating, Ma said, "You'd best go right to bed. Pa worked you awful hard in the corn patch today."

Pa choked on his coffee, but he didn't say anything. Jamey went to his room and waited until he thought his parents were asleep, then he sneaked into the pantry and felt around in the darkness until he found a sack. He slipped a dozen biscuits into the sack, then some cheese and the rest of the fried chicken.

He couldn't sleep after he went back to his room. He lay on his side staring out of the window into the blackness, seeing himself on his white horse with the entire regiment behind him. Custer, or Sully, or perhaps even Sheridan, if he took the field personally, would come to him and ask, "What's your advice, Colonel Burns? Shall we try to flank them?"

"Sir," he would answer haughtily, "never mention a flanking movement to Colonel Burns. We'll break their backs with a charge."

The bugle would sound and the band would play and he'd draw his saber and order, "Charge." There would be five thousand warriors massed in front of him: Cheyennes, Sioux, Arapahoes, Kiowas, Comanches, and Apaches. But numbers wouldn't do them any good. They'd see him astride his white horse, his flashing saber in his hand, and their hearts would fail them. All the pleadings of brave chiefs like Roman Nose and Dull Knife would not hold the savages in line.

From that day on, the history books would recite how Colonel Burns had smashed the power of the plains Indians with a single charge. He felt sorry for Sheridan and Hancock and Sully and Custer. They'd be crowded clean off the pages of history.

He woke with a start. It was almost daylight. He must have gone to sleep after all. He picked up his sack of food, then remembered he hadn't written a note to Ma. He found a scrap of paper and pencil and wrote: "Dear Ma. I'm not going to waste my life in a corn patch. I'm going to fight Indians. Your son. Jim Burns."

He left the paper on his bed where Ma would find it and slipped out through the window, wishing he'd done this months ago. He saddled his gelding, tied the sack behind the cantle, and led the horse out of the yard. He hadn't expected to get this far. He mounted and rode away slowly, thinking that every minute Pa would come roaring after him and make him go back.

An hour later he heard a rider behind him and pulled off to the side of the road. Pa wasn't going to take him back. That's all there was to it.

But it wasn't Pa after all. It was Mr. Jones, riding his big sorrel Reddy nice and easy the way he always did. Jamey said, "Howdy, Mr. Jones."

Jedediah pulled up. "What are you doing here, Jamey? It's not full daylight yet."

"I'm going away," Jamey said. "Did Ma send you after me?"

A funny little grin worried the corners of Jedediah's mouth the way it did sometimes when he was tickled about something but didn't think it was polite to come right out and laugh. "No, Jamey. I'm going to Fort Hays."

Jamey sighed. He hoped it sounded as if he were relieved. He said, "I'll ride along with you. That's where I'm going."

Jedediah frowned. "Your folks don't know you're leaving?"

"No, sir. All Pa thinks I can do is to hoe corn. Well, I've been doing some dreaming like you said to. I aim to join the Army and stop this Indian trouble."

The little grin threatened again, then faded, and Jedediah was frowning. "It's going to take more than dreaming to stop the Indian trouble. You'd better turn around and go home."

"No, sir." He chewed his lower lip, surprised that Mr. Jones would talk this way. "If you won't let me ride with you, I'll just have to follow you."

"Go back home," Jedediah said curtly. "This is man's business."

"I'm a man," Jamey said angrily. "I'm the best shot in the county next to you."

"Your coming in second at the turkey shoot last Thanksgiving didn't exactly prove that," Jedediah said. "I haven't got time to hog-tie you and take you home. I'm just telling you."

He put his sorrel into a gallop and went on down the road. Jamey followed, furiously angry and disappointed. If Mr. Jones didn't want to ride with him, all right. Jamey would keep him in sight. He wasn't exactly sure how to get to Fort Hays, but he'd make him take him there whether he wanted to or not.

Mr. Jones would be sorry he'd acted this way when he read the newspapers after the campaign was over, mighty sorry.

Chapter 8

JEDEDIAH had been assigned three o'clock guard duty with Deacon Andy Crowell. When it was time, he woke Crowell and they replaced the sentries on the south side of the camp. Redig remained by the fire and Harney continued to snore.

Jedediah paced back and forth, a short walk between the sentry west of him and Crowell on the east. Occasionally he stopped to talk with one of them and then walked again, his loaded carbine in his hands.

Nothing changed as the pit-black minutes dragged by: the night sounds, the chill wind that bit into a man, and the thoughts. Always the thoughts, one spawning another. Of Cally. Of Jamey Burns, who should never have come. Of Matthew Redig and Bill Harney. Of old injuries received and injuries given, of hopes and plans and ambitions, none of them seeming very important now.

His ears were straining to catch the slightest whisper of an enemy slithering through the grass; his eyes tried to probe the blackness, but he could see nothing. An overcast had spread across the sky, hiding even the few stars that had given out their feeble light earlier in the evening.

He seemed to have two distinct sections in his mind: the one that was on guard duty at this moment, the other alive with the past, his thoughts and memories continually searching and twisting and seeking. Finally he dredged his father up from the distant years, a painful memory he wished he could forget.

He had a clear mental picture of his father, a handsome man as tall as he was now, but heavier in his arms and shoulders. He remembered their Missouri farm and the small house his father kept as well as any woman could; the bands of border ruffians that rode by at night on their way to Kansas, and the stories of bloodshed that came to them. He remembered the heated arguments in the country store where his father traded, and his father always outside the circle of men as he listened to the talk about slaves and states' rights and secession, an amused smile on his lean face.

He remembered, too, the trip across the plains to Colorado, PIKES PEAK OR BUST written in tall, black letters on their wagon; the village that was Denver, and the fruitless search for gold. He had often asked himself if his father had ever cared deeply for anything until he met the woman, anything but the books he had brought to Colorado which seemed more important to him than the gold he never found.

Jedediah had forgotten the woman's name, but he remembered how she looked, tall and very pretty. She lived in the cabin next to theirs on Cherry Creek, and he remembered how she stood in the doorway smiling at his father when he came home late in the afternoon, and he remembered his father's face, more animated than he had ever seen it before in his life. He remembered coming home one evening from his job in a stable and finding his father and the team and the wagon gone, and a neighbor telling him they had left that morning, his father and the woman.

Here the remembering stopped, as if a great black gate had slammed shut in his mind, and there were no memories for a time except the pain and fear and the desperate hope that his father would come back. But he never did, and somehow Jedediah survived.

Eventually he began living again. If he had been older and wiser, he might have understood. He might even have forgiven his father, but he had been only fourteen. The bitterness and the heartache remained, scarring him so deeply that he feared love more than physical danger, feared it so much that he had refused Cally. Now it was too late to tell her he was sorry, too late to tell her anything at all.

What should a man think of in the hours before he died? Jedediah was not afraid of hell. He was not even afraid of the unknown. If there was a life after death, a man would learn to live it just as he learned to live this one. He believed there was a God, but he could not accept the puny God Who seemed so real to Andy Crowell.

He reached the eastern end of his walk, Crowell's squat figure looming out of the darkness ahead of him; he heard Crowell say, "Slim."

"See anything, Andy?"

"Nothing." Crowell hesitated, then he said, "Slim, you were there when I left home. You know why I came."

"Yes, I know."

"I should of done something to make Jamey go home. But I didn't, and what's worse is that I've failed with the men. I've tried to talk to them, but they won't listen. Harney says we're all going to die tomorrow. Why won't they listen at a time like this?"

"A man never has ears for something he doesn't want to hear," Jedediah said. "Some of them will listen when they're ready for it."

"Then it will be too late," Crowell said mournfully.

As he turned to pace the other way, Jedediah felt a deep sympathy for Andy Crowell. He was carrying the weight of fifty lost souls upon his back.

Chapter 9

ANDY Crowell paced slowly along the edge of the camp, his gloomy thoughts on the men whose souls he had tried to save. He had talked to Matthew Redig for an hour at a time, but the man acted as if he didn't hear a word Crowell said. Bill Harney wouldn't even listen. If any man needed to repent of his sins, it was Braggin' Bill Harney. His life was filled with sin: drunkenness and fighting and adultery. Jedediah Jones was even worse, in the sense that he knew better than to go on living unsaved the way he was, but the Lord had not opened Jedediah's heart to Crowell's words.

He didn't know what he could do that he hadn't done. He'd tried right from the day the command had left Fort Hays, but he'd failed. He remembered how he had felt the morning he'd left home with no thought of failure in his mind. If there had been, he would have stayed home. No, the prospect of failure had not occurred to him; he had been certain he would reap a great harvest for the Lord, and that would bring him a fitting reward when the Day of Judgment came.

On the morning of August 28 Andy Crowell woke at dawn as he always did. He eased out of bed, not wanting to wake his wife and start her tongue going so early. He glanced at her as he gathered up his clothes. Although he could not make out her face clearly in the thin light, he knew exactly how she looked: her gray hair spilling over the pillow, the row of whiskers above her mouth, her lips fluttering with every snore.

Everything that Sadie Crowell did was on the magnificent side, and that included her snoring. When she was on her back, she was the equal of a complete band composed of wind instruments, none of them in tune. She was a wonderful cook, a fastidious housekeeper, and as good a hand with a breaking plow as any man in the Laura's Tit community.

He slipped out of the bedroom, seeking refuge as he always did in the knowledge that the Lord gave every man a cross to bear, and his was Sadie. Sometimes when the cross was so heavy he thought he could not bear it, he pondered the Lord's reason and decided it was a test. Being a spiritual leader, he would be given the heaviest cross of anyone, so he must make his life an example for others; he must be a great rock holding firm against all temptations, a rock of the Lord.

Dressed, he took the milk bucket from the pantry and slipped out through the back door. Sadie would wake up in time to build the fire and cook breakfast, often having to wait for him if he communed too long with the Lord. When that happened, she made a few opening remarks that sharpened up her tongue, then she turned it loose for the day. According to her, he wasted his time acting as if he were something special. Well, he sure wasn't, she said. He should stay home and do his share of the work. If he did, she wouldn't have to spend half her time in the field the way she did. He felt sorry for her. She just didn't understand.

He entered the barn and, hanging his bucket on a peg in the wall, climbed to the mow and lay down in the hay. He did this every morning, for this was the time of quiet when God spoke to him.

Sometimes the Lord gave him specific directions. He would say, "Andy, go to the Tilton home and pray with Ruth. The sins of the flesh in the form of Jamey Burns are a great temptation to her." Or, "Call on the Burns family. None of them are saved and Link Burns is a drunkard and a brawler. Show him the path to salvation." Or, "Jedediah Jones is a man of knowledge, but he is prideful. The road to hell is lined with the souls of proud men."

Sometimes the results were miraculous, as when he called on the Tiltons and prayed with Ruth. She was repentant and he assured her parents that she was saved. On the other hand, he failed miserably with the Burns family. He had to leave on the run, his short legs pumping for all they were worth, Link Burns solemnly warning him that if he wasn't off Burns land in thirty seconds he would personally tear him limb from limb. He had done little better with Jedediah Jones, who was cynical and lost in self-pride.

This morning he knew the Lord was trying to tell him something, but the message couldn't seem to get through. He lay there until the sun was up, staring at the little stars of light which showed between the shakes on the roof, but for some reason he just couldn't hear the Lord this morning. He finally went back down the ladder and did the chores. He had failed, but he would remain aware of the Lord's presence all day, and perhaps he would get the word later.

He felt very humble as he walked to the house with the milk bucket in his hand, the foam high above the rim. Sadie was standing at the stove frying ham when he came in, an apron tied around her ample waist. She looked at him and sniffed, a disdainful sound that in one second completely wiped out his spiritual mood.

"A body would like to know how you can take so long to milk one cow," Sadie said. "I declare, Andrew, I wished I'd married a bucket of molasses and moved to the north pole. I could have got it to move faster'n you do."

He hurried into the pantry and set the bucket down, praying silently for strength to bear this plague of words which Sadie visited upon him every day. He returned to the kitchen to wash, Sadie going on in her strident voice, "You've got to get into the garden today or the weeds will take it. You know as well as I do that most of our winter's living comes out of the garden."

He heard someone call from the yard and hurried outside, thankful for even a short respite. Jedediah Jones sat his big sorrel, his thin face showing more concern than Andy had ever seen it show. Usually the teacher seemed kind of stand-offish to Andy, as if he didn't care about anybody but himself, but this morning he was plainly worried.

" 'Morning, Slim," Andy said. "Git down and have breakfast with us."

Jedediah glanced back along the road in the direction from which he had come, then he said, "Be glad to, Andy, but first I'd better tell you that I stopped for some help. I'm going to Fort Hays to join Forsyth's scouts and I've got Jamey Burns hanging to my tail. He's bound to follow me, claiming he's going to enlist in the Army, but he'll never make a soldier. Besides, his folks will have a fit."

Andy considered that a moment, then he asked, "Want me to tell his folks?"

"No, damn it. I want you to talk to him. It's not right, going off this way. His folks need him."

Andy squinted against the early morning sun, deciding the vengeance of the Lord was being visited upon Link Burns. "Well, I dunno about his help being needed. If his Pa wasn't a drunkard and a brawler, he could do all the work there is to do on that farm."

Jedediah glanced back and saw that Jamey was turning in from the road. He said, "That's not the point. Jamey's just a fool kid who does a lot of dreaming, but he hasn't got anything to back it up. I couldn't make him go home. Maybe you can."

"Let me think on it," Andy said, and called to Jamey, "Come on in, son. Breakfast is on the table."

Jamey dismounted with alacrity. "That sure sounds good, Mr. Crowell."

As Andy turned toward the back door, he saw Jedediah dismount, his face showing his irritation. Andy hurried into the kitchen. He said, "Put two more plates on, Sadie. Jedediah Jones and the Burns boy just rode in."

Sadie licked her lips, then said, "Of all the gall I ever seen in my born days . . ." She stopped as Jamey Burns came in through the back door, Jedediah automatically ducking his head as he followed. "Come right in, Mr. Jones. You, too, Jamey. I'll set a couple of plates before you can say scat."

"We don't want to put you out any, ma'am," Jedediah said.

"Why, pshaw, you ain't putting me out none," she said. "No indeedy."

Something was tugging at Andy's mind, something vague that wouldn't quite take shape, but he had a haunting feeling it was important. After they started to eat, he said to Jedediah, "What's this about Forsyth's scouts? I ain't heard nothing about 'em."

Jedediah frowned and didn't answer until he had drunk his coffee. He glanced at Jamey, who was watching him, then he said, "You haven't talked to Jamey yet."

"No, and I'm not going to," Andy said. "I've been thinking on it and I've decided the boy's better off in the Army than he is at home. I went there one day to talk to Link Burns about salvation and I almost didn't get away alive. I guess he was drunk."

Jamey snickered. "Pa said he never seen a short-legged man run so fast."

Andy was five feet, six inches tall, with an abnormally long body and legs that were, in sharp contrast, abnormally short. He sat back, glaring at Jamey. "Your Pa had no right to do what he done, with me going there to do the Lord's work."

"They crucified Jesus," Jedediah said. "All the apostles except John died a violent death. Aren't you willing to follow their example?"

Sadie laughed. "I sure admire the way you talk, Mr. Jones. They do say all over the district that it stretches a man's brains just to listen to you."

Andy ignored her. He said to Jedediah, "I would willingly die serving the Lord if that is what He wants me to do, but the question is what's best for the boy. I admire his spunk

47

in wanting to join the Army. Now, I asked about Forsyth's scouts."

"I don't know the details," Jedediah said, "but I understand that Sheridan has commissioned Forsyth to enlist fifty civilian scouts who will move immediately into the Indian country."

Jamey stared at him, wide-eyed. "I won't join the Army," he said. "I'll join the scouts you're talking about."

Jedediah groaned. "Jamey, I told you once this is man's work."

"He'll never be a man if he don't get a chance to prove it," Andy said. "He's big and he's strong. He's a good shot and he can handle a horse. I'll vouch for him, if you won't."

Then it came to Andy, the message the Lord had been trying to get through to him that morning. Here were men going out to fight, many of them to die. Here were souls waiting to be harvested for the Lord.

Andy finished his coffee and rose. "I'm going with you," he said.

Sadie was standing by the stove. Now she looked as if she had been struck a physical blow. As Andy walked past her toward the door, she grabbed him by the arm, crying out, "Have you gone daft? Isn't it enough for you to go sashaying around over the country shirking your work and leaving it to me to do, without going off and fighting Indians? Maybe you'll get killed and I'll be a widow."

Andy looked at her, thinking this was the first sign of weakness he had seen in her since they were married. He said, "You can take care of things till I get back. I am not Jonah refusing to go to Nineveh."

He jerked free from her grasp and went out, Sadie screaming at him, "You're just a dirty, scrubby-faced little man. The Lord won't even claim you when the Judgment Day comes."

She turned her back to Jedediah and Jamey, who were still at the table, and began to cry. Jedediah rose, and going to Sadie, awkwardly patted her on a shoulder. "Don't worry about him, Mrs. Crowell. He'll come back."

She whirled on Jedediah, tears running down her weathered cheeks. "For what? To go on neglecting me and the farm while he coyotes around tending to everybody's business but his own? He's bald-headed, but I hope to God some Injun can find enough hair to scalp him."

"I guess you don't mean that," Jedediah said.

"Sure I mean it," she flung at him. "He'll never change. I ain't gonna keep on fooling myself about it."

Jedediah jerked his head at Jamey and the boy followed him outside. Jedediah said, "I guess I can't keep you from going to Fort Hays, but you'd better be sure you understand one thing. It takes more than dreams to be a scout."

Jamey dug a boot toe through the dust, then forced himself to look at Jedediah. "I'll remember."

Andy had saddled his horse. Now he mounted and the three of them left the yard and turned toward Fort Hays.

They were a mile down the road before Andy remembered he hadn't kissed Sadie good-bye. Well, she hadn't expected it. Come to think of it, he couldn't remember the last time he had kissed her. With that thought, his conscience ceased to trouble him, and the spiritual mood was in him again as he considered the opportunity the Lord was giving him.

Chapter 10

JEDEDIAH judged that it was about an hour before dawn when he stopped his pacing, every nerve in his body jangling a warning. He stood motionless, his carbine on the ready, his eyes trying to pierce the darkness, and failing. He was certain he had seen something move, but now he wondered if it had been his imagination.

He moved silently across the grass toward where he thought he had seen the movement, thinking that if it was an Indian snaking his way toward the picket line to steal the horses, he would get a bullet or a knife before he knew what was happening. But it might be a scout trying to leave camp, so he couldn't just shoot and ask questions later.

He was on the man before he realized it, almost stepping on him. The fellow was belly-flat on the ground, motionless and silent, apparently depending on the darkness to hide him. Jedediah jammed the muzzle of his Spencer into the man's back.

"Identify yourself," he said softly.

"Harney." Keeping his voice down, he cursed bitterly, then he said, "Pull that gun out of my back. By God, Jed, you've got eyes like a cat or you'd never have spotted me. I thought I was clean away."

Jedediah stepped back, keeping his carbine on the big man. Filled with a quick and unreasonable fury, he said, "I ought to kill you, Bill. There might be some excuse for a kid like Jamey Burns to run, but not for a man like you."

"You're wrong, friend," Harney said. "Jamey wouldn't last the day out, but I'd get through. I'd go to Fort Wallace and send help back. Before this is finished, you'll wish to hell you'd have let me go, if you're still alive when it's finished."

"You'll go when Forsyth sends you," Jedediah said. "Not when you decide to sneak off like the yellow bastard Redig says you are."

"I ain't yellow," Harney said. "I'm just smarter'n anybody else in camp. It's my guess that in an hour or two the Injuns will make a try at our horses. After that nobody'll get away."

"I don't think you had any idea of going for help," Jedediah said. "You don't think of anything except your own hide."

"I'd have sent help back, all right," Harney said cheerfully, "only it wouldn't have done any good. They wouldn't find nuthin' 'cept some carcasses rottin' in the sun. Or just the bones the coyotes left."

"Get up and go back to the camp," Jedediah said. "I don't see how you got past me."

"Went right between you and Crowell. I've wiggled out o' Indian camps, so this wasn't no trick, though I don't know how you ever spotted me."

Jedediah wasn't sure himself. It must have been a delayed reaction to Harney's movement through the grass or some small sound that had been slow to register in his mind. But whatever it was, he had the man. He had no more patience with Harney. Deserting the group of which he was a member was to Jedediah the rankest kind of cowardice, and now he knew he could shoot Harney without the slightest hesitation if he made a move to escape.

"Get back to camp," Jedediah said. "I won't tell you again."

"Sure," Harney said agreeably. Still, he seemed to feel the need to defend himself, and he added, "I should o' done this last night 'cause I knew what was comin'. I tried to talk you into savin' your hide, but you're too damned noble. Well, tonight I laid there thinkin' it was crazy for us to stay here and get butchered like a bunch of sheep. Trouble was, I should of done it before you went on guard. Nobody else would o' nailed me."

Jedediah wondered why Harney had waited as long as he had. He wouldn't have gone far in an hour. Then it occurred to Jedediah that the man was planning to angle toward the picket line and take his horse. Once mounted, he could have gone a long way in an hour. Forsyth would not have been likely to have ordered a pursuit. So, unless the Indians had the column surrounded, Harney would probably have made it.

"How did you get past Redig?" Jedediah asked.

"Looked to me like he was asleep. He was sittin' there at the fire with his head down."

"Move." Jedediah prodded him with his rifle. "We'll have another guard on us in a minute. If Forsyth or McCall hears about this, you'll get shot."

"You mean you ain't tellin' 'em?"

"Just get back to camp."

Suddenly it struck Jedediah that Harney fully expected to be shot, that in the face of that danger he had been cool enough. He wasn't a coward. As he saw it, he was a realist and everybody else was foolish.

Crowell appeared out of the darkness, asking in a low voice, "What's going on?"

Jedediah hesitated, then he said, "Harney was making a break. If he tries it again, we'll shoot him."

Crowell sighed. "If we didn't need every rifle we've got, I'd say shoot him anyway. I reckon Forsyth better not know."

A moment later, with Harney in camp, Jedediah resumed his pacing. He asked himself the same question about Harney he had asked about every man in the column: Why had he joined?

Chapter 11

BILL HARNEY rolled up in his blanket, but he did not sleep. He'd had so many dates with death that he couldn't remember how he'd got out of all of them, but this one was going to be the tightest if he made it, and right now he had a hunch he wouldn't.

Harney had never considered himself stupid, but he guessed he must be, at that. Any man was foolish who put his life in the hands of a God-damned popinjay with brass buttons on his coat who couldn't think of anything but getting a promotion. He knew the Army, so he couldn't blame anyone but himself for getting into this mess, although at the time it had seemed the smart thing to do. Well, it wasn't the first mistake he'd made, but it sure could be the last.

Now there was nothing to do but lie here and stare at the stars and curse himself for ever joining the outfit in the first place.

Braggin' Bill Harney was almost broke when he rode into Hays City in the afternoon of August 28, but he wasn't worried. Phil Sheridan was likely at the fort, and the chances were Harney could talk the General into giving him a scout's job. He looked the part, and that helped. He stood six four, with shoulders that were both wide and thick; he wore buckskin, his hair was down to his shoulders, and his brows were bristling awnings over his dark eyes. He never went without his revolver and bowie knife.

He'd buy himself a restaurant meal, have a drink, maybe work up a fight just to make the day interesting, and then he'd go to the fort and look Sheridan up. Of course he'd be choosey about the fight he picked. He never took on a man he didn't think he could lick, although there were times when he had to extend himself if his victim had two or three friends. But he was well satisfied if it took three or four men to whip him. At least he could prove that at fifty he was a better man than most who were half his age.

He hadn't been in Hays City for a while, but he wasn't surprised by what he saw. The end of steel was far to the west now, having moved from Hays City to Coyote, then Monument, and was now at Sheridan, not far from Fort Wallace. Much of Hays City had gone west with the end of track, but Main Street was still flanked with saloons, gambling halls, and brothels, enough of a town to satisfy him.

He reined up in front of the Dew Drop Inn Saloon, tied his horse, and looked along Main Street. Not much sign of what some men called progress, and that pleased him. He hated progress; it destroyed his way of life everywhere it went.

Main Street was wide, the dust up to a horse's hocks, the sun hammering down as if it knew there weren't many days left after August to fry the juices out of a man. Horses were tied at the hitch rails, a few wagons and rigs were scattered in front of the saloons, and here and there he saw knots of men taking advantage of a skinny patch of shade to stand and talk.

He turned into the saloon, wondering if he was smart to ask for a scout's job. Sheridan might order a winter campaign after the way the red devils had been raising hell on the Saline and Solomon rivers. A man could get mighty cold on a winter campaign. But winter was a long ways off. He'd worry about it when the time came.

Walking to the bar, he ordered whisky and looked around. Here were the usual kinds of men he would expect to find in a town like Hays City: wolfers, buffalo hunters, soldiers from the fort, businessmen, gamblers, con men, pimps from the brothels on down the street, and the inevitable dreamy-eyed homesteaders asking for information about two things in particular: the location of good land and the Indian danger.

One of them stood at Harney's right. He was complaining. It was Harney's observation that homesteaders were a breed of failures always looking for something for nothing, and it was their nature to bitch about one thing or another.

"I got into town yesterday," the man said. "I put my family up in a hotel, but I'll go broke keeping 'em there and buying meals for 'em. I've got to find me a piece of land."

A little man who stood on the other side of the homesteader was a sharpshooter with a derby hat, a diamond stick pin, and a boiled shirt. He reminded Harney of a hound dog sniffing a scent. He had a fox's eyes, a gopher's mouth, and a nose that kept twitching like a rabbit's. Harney didn't hate many men on sight, but he hated this one, the reason being that he had been taken a few times by men very much like this one.

"I can fix you up afore night, Mr. Garvey," the little man said. "We'll go get my buggy and I'll show you the best quarter section of bottom land that ever graced God's glorious out-of-doors."

"I ain't got much money," the homesteader said dubiously. "Just enough to buy a team and wagon and enough grub to last till I can get a crop."

"That's all you need in Kansas, Mr. Garvey," the little man said. "But be sure you buy land that has been proved up on. This farm I have in mind is just right for you. House ready to move into. A shed for your team. Close to town where there's a school and a church. Some of the sod already broken."

Harney saw that the homesteader was almost convinced. He tapped the man on the shoulder. He said, "Friend, ask this yahoo how many times your crops will be washed out by a flood before you harvest one."

The little man's face turned red. He blurted, "Keep your fat nose out of this, mister."

"You're bein' headed for the pen to be sheared like an innercent lamb," Harney said. "It's my hunch that this son-of-a-bitch is fixin' to sell you a piece of land that floods every spring. Chances are he's in cahoots with the bank and they've sold this farm seventeen times."

The little man quivered with rage. He screamed, "Clay, come here!"

Harney turned to see a big man bearing down on him. He was going to have his fight, all right, but not with the sharpshooter. He pounded the bar and yelled, "Come on, Clay. I'm half man, half alligator. I can outcuss, outfight, and outdrink any ten men in Hays City if they're like you and your pipsqueak of a partner."

Clay stopped two paces away, not sure whether Harney was all brag or not. The man in the derby squealed, "Bust him up, Clay. Damn it, what am I paying you for?"

Clay took a half-hearted swing, plainly not liking the prospect of a fight with Harney. He missed and Harney hit him once in the soft part of the belly, then on the chin, and Clay was finished. Harney turned in time to see the man in the derby jerk a derringer out of his pocket. The homesteader had disappeared.

The little man was slow and Harney caught his wrist, twisted the derringer from his hand, and laid it on the bar, then he picked the man up with one hand and held him dangling, his brightly polished shoes two feet off the floor.

"I've got a mind to jam that cap pistol of your'n down your throat," Harney said. "You ain't much man. You're just a gnat buzzin' in my ear."

The sharpshooter kicked and cursed and yelled, "Let me go! Let me go!"

"Sure, you can go," Bill said amiably.

He tossed the little man toward the center of the room as he might have tossed a wiggling pup. The man staggered, tried to get his balance, and failed. He sprawled backward over a poker table, upsetting it and sending cards and money cascading to the floor.

Harney laughed at the commotion he had created. Men swore and threatened to throw the little man out of the place, then a big freighter shouted, "It ain't his fault. It's the big gent there at the bar."

Another man yelled, "Get the marshal!"

A third said, "Naw, it's time somebody took care of Honest George. It'll smell better in here if we throw him out."

By the time the table was set upright and the money and the cards picked up, Honest George had left and was back with the town marshal, a lanky man with a handlebar mustache, a pair of bone-handled revolvers on his hip, and a gold star on his vest.

Harney quit laughing and considered this development. He didn't know the marshal, so he wasn't sure how to proceed. Some of the frontier law men were bluffs, some were tough, and Harney had no desire to go to jail if he made the wrong guess on this one.

"You're under arrest for disturbing the peace," the marshal said. "Give me your gun."

"You're makin' a mistake, Marshal," Harney said. "All I done was to bust up a scheme of that there pint-sized varmint they call Honest George."

"Let me have your gun," the marshal said. "We've got a judge who's paid to listen to stories like yours."

"You aimin' to haul me off to your calaboose?"

"Them are my intentions," the marshal admitted.

Harney scratched a bearded cheek. The marshal's eyes, half closed, were two pieces of agate; his right hand was close to the butt of his gun. No brag in this one, Harney decided, but to be locked up in jail with its lice and stink and tiny cell so small a man couldn't rightly scratch himself was more than he could stand. He was a fair hand with a gun. He just might take the marshal, if it came to that.

"In no way have I done wrong," Harney said earnestly. "If you've lived in the same burg with this here Honest

George, you ought to know the kind of shenanigan he was up to."

"I'm not the judge or jury," the marshal snapped, "but by God, I ain't standing here augering with you."

"And you ain't lockin' me up," Harney said. "If'n you try, you'll wind up in a doc's office and he'll be wonderin' if you got chewed by a catamount."

A man who had been standing behind Harney watching the scene stepped forward and nodded at the marshal. "What this man says is true, Hank. Will you let him go if I agree to get him out of town?"

The law man scratched his nose as Honest George let out a wail of protest. The newcomer said, "George, someday you're going to get stepped on and squashed like a bug. Now shut up."

"All right, Mr. Pliley," the marshal said, "but I'll tell you this. If he ain't out of town in an hour, I'll throw him into the jug so long he'll trip on his beard every time he takes a step."

"I understand," Pliley said.

Harney shook hands with Pliley after the marshal and Honest George left the saloon. He said, "Thank you kindly. I was honin' for a fight, but not with the law." He looked Pliley over, then asked, "Ain't you the one who scouted for the Army at Beaver Creek last year?"

"I'm the man," Pliley said. "You're Braggin' Bill Harney, aren't you?"

"Keerect," Harney said. "Well, sir, it's a pleasure to meet you. Got plugged a couple of times at Beaver Creek, I heered."

"Twice in the leg," Pliley said. "Bullets went in three inches apart." He squinted at Harney speculatively, then asked, "Working?"

"No. I figgered I'd see if Sheridan needed a scout."

"Fine." Pliley slapped him on the back. "The Army needs fifty of them, and you'll just about make the fiftieth man if we get a move on."

"What kind of a campaign is Sheridan figgerin' on, takin' fifty scouts?"

"This is a special bunch," Pliley said. "Sheridan commissioned Colonel Forsyth to enlist fifty men for active duty. Now let's get out to the fort before he signs up some farmer who can't shoot."

Harney followed Pliley out of the saloon, grinning as he thought about this. He might have been dead by now, or in jail, which could have been worse. As he mounted his horse, he said, "Well, sir, you just never know how a man's stick is gonna float, now do you?"

Chapter 12

THE OVERCAST that had covered the sky earlier in the night broke away and Jedediah was aware that the stars had come out again, making a faint glow all down the long slope of the sky to the horizon. Dawn was no more than a few minutes away.

Jedediah remembered how the sunrise had been in the Colorado high country, the mountains on the east remaining in deep shadow while those on the west caught and held the first golden thrust of the sun. But here there were no mountains, just the everlasting sweep of the sky and the land running on and on until they met, the only break in the monotony the long ridge to the south with an occasional swell bulging against the sky, and the low bluffs on the north.

Forsyth joined Jedediah and walked beside him, saying bleakly, "If they're going to make a try for our horses, they'll do it soon." He paused, then asked, "Have you seen or heard anything, Jones?"

Jedediah hesitated, considering the possibility that Forsyth might have made an accurate guess about Braggin' Bill Harney's attempt to escape. He said, "I've heard some coyotes. An owl once in a while. I wouldn't make a bet that some of it didn't come from an Indian."

"Quite possible," Forsyth said, and continued to pace beside Jedediah.

Forsyth, Jedediah knew, had slept little, if any, during the night. He had made more than one circle of the camp, pausing to speak with one guard after another. He had been with Crowell only a moment before. He lingered here, Jedediah thought, because he was near the picket line.

If Forsyth felt the slightest touch of physical fear, he did not show it. Still, Jedediah wondered about the thoughts that were running through his mind. Did he have any regrets about leading his command this far from Fort

Wallace with rations nearly gone? Had he now recognized the insanity of the odds, fifty men against at least five hundred? Had he finally realized that promotion for a dead brevet colonel came too late?

Probably not, Jedediah decided. Forsyth was too calm, too confident of his destiny and that of his command. Regardless of his mental reservations of Forsyth's judgment, Jedediah could not discount the man's cold courage. But courage by itself was not enough.

For a brief moment Jedediah questioned his own wisdom in turning Harney back; then he told himself he had been right. This was not a question of emotional involvement; it was one of plain common sense, of survival. The decision had been made back there at Fort Hays three weeks ago, a decision that was final and irrevocable.

Now the first hint of dawn showed in the sky, gradually diming the stars. The night air, chill and biting, breathed down the creek and made a faint rustling sound in the brush on the island. Jedediah shivered, conscious of the touch of the cold metal of the Spencer in his hand.

He wondered, as he had so many times during the past hours, how the men could sleep on this, of all nights. Perhaps they weren't sleeping; perhaps they were lying tense and motionless in their blankets, waiting for the sun, nerves pulled tight as they waited for the pound of unshod hoofs upon the grass, the terrifying screech of Indian yells.

Suddenly a nerve-jangling warning came to Jedediah just as it had an hour ago when he discovered Harney trying to escape. A sound this time, the whispered drop of a horse's hoofs into the mat of grass that covered the prairie. Forsyth heard it, too, for his hand touched Jedediah's left arm briefly, then he dropped it and they moved closer to the picket line.

A moment later Jedediah glimpsed the fluttering feathers of a war bonnet as a mounted brave appeared over a rise in the land and was silhouetted against the brightening sky. He felt his heart give one great thumping beat as other warriors appeared. He didn't know how many there were as he brought his Spencer to his shoulder and squeezed off a shot at the first brave he had seen. Forsyth fired a second later.

"Indians!" Forsyth yelled. "Turn out. Indians!"

Instantly hell broke out in front of them. Noise slammed against Jedediah's ears as he ran toward his sorrel; the rump-tightening yells that could come only from Indian throats, the beating of drums, the rattling of dry hides. There was this moment of chaotic confusion as the Indians waved blankets in their frantic efforts to stampede the horses and pack mules, then the men poured from the camp toward the picket line.

Shots hammered into the hideous racket the Indians were making. Frightened horses squealed and plunged and kicked in their frantic efforts to break loose. A few succeeded and raced up the valley on the dead run, the Indians right behind them, still screaming and waving blankets.

Jedediah reached his sorrel and, grabbing the lariat, talked to the animal as he tried to quiet him. Other men had their horses' ropes by that time, bringing some semblance of order out of the confusion.

Forsyth shouted, "Saddle and stand to horse." In a matter of seconds the horses were bridled and saddled, then the men were standing in line, reins in their left hands, loaded rifles on the ready.

"They got seven of 'em," Sharp Grover yelled from somewhere on down the line.

Excitement had hit Jedediah like a great tidal wave, making him react more from instinct than from conscious direction. The sense of immediate danger was past and suddenly a great fist of fury closed over his heart as he thought of the seven stolen horses, and he felt as if he had been sucked into a whirling pool as he remembered Cally's words, "Is there anything you love except your horse?"

He stood with Crowell on one side and Jamey Burns on the other, his breath coming in hard, gusty pants. For the first time in his life he hated someone, hated the Indians in that raiding party, hated them with a depth of emotion he had not realized he was capable of feeling. Suppose the Indians had stolen his sorrel along with the other seven?

He slipped a hand over Reddy's neck, and stood there, trembling and sweating in the chill air as he waited for the next order. He wanted to kill Cheyennes, a compelling desire that went beyond reason. For the first time he thought he understood how Matthew Redig felt.

Part Two
THE BATTLE

Chapter 13

THE opalescent dawn light steadily deepened until the ridge lines to the north and south were visible. Harney, standing at his horse's head next to Jedediah, asked, "What do you suppose Colonel Brass Buttons will do? If we take off down the creek, they'll close in and wipe us out."

A moment later Jedediah heard Sharp Grover say, "My God, Colonel, look at the Indians!"

Jedediah saw them just as Grover spoke. He had been expecting to see Indians for the last twenty-four hours, but he had not counted on anything like this. They seemed to spring up out of the earth. They were all around the command: upstream and downstream from them, on both sides of the creek, on the bluffs to the north, mounted men moving like wraiths through the dim, ghostly light.

It was enough to see them, hundreds of them, maybe a thousand, but it was worse to hear them: their terrifying war cries, the banging of their drums, their death songs chanted with savage exultation that was different from anything Jedediah had ever heard in his life. The short hairs on the back of his neck felt as if they were standing straight out, and again that chill went up and down his spine.

The Indians poured toward the column from all sides like an engulfing flood, feathers fluttering in the chill dawn breeze, each warrior practically naked except for his paint and regalia of war. It was a terrifying sight to Jedediah, savage and magnificent, and deadly. The thought knifed through his consciousness that he would never see Cally again.

"We're surrounded!" Jamey screamed. "They'll kill every one of us!"

Panicky, the boy would have mounted and raced away to certain death if Jedediah had not called out, "Hold it, Jamey. We can make out if we get on the island."

Jedediah wasn't sure whether Forsyth heard, or whether he thought of it himself. In either case, the welcome com-

mand came down the line, "Reach the island and dig in."
The order was picked up and repeated by Beecher and
McCall, and instantly every man mounted and broke for
the island.

No order now, just a wild, crazy rush like that of a flock
of frightened chickens for the hen house when a hawk
swoops overhead. Jedediah felt Reddy break over the crum-
bling south bank and hit the soft sand of the stream bed,
flounder and almost lose his footing, and then recover.
Water flew from his hoofs in a silver spray as he struck
the shallow flow in the middle of the creek, then he was
floundering again in the dry sand. A great lunge carried him
out of the stream bed onto the island that was covered by
tall grass, weeds, and low-growing brush.

Jedediah reined up, dismounted, and tied Reddy to a
clump of willows. As other men rushed past, he heard the
shouted command, "Dig in. Dig in." He obeyed, slashing
frantically with his butcher knife through the covering of
grass and scooping the sand out of the hole with his tin
plate. He was aware of a change in the tone of the Indian
yells to one of dismay and anger, and perhaps frustration.

Harney, digging beside Jedediah, was as calm as if this
were no more than the making of a night camp. "They
thought they had us," he called to Jedediah, "but they
didn't allow for this. If they'd grabbed the island afore
they showed theirselves, we'd be goners sure."

No time to dig a real trench, no time to see what was
happening to Jamey or Andy Crowell or anyone else.
Scoop with the tin plate, cut and slash the grass and roots
with the butcher knife, while all the time bullets and arrows
were flying overhead, hitting the horses and knocking them
to earth. Now and then Jedediah heard a yell of agony as
a man was hit.

He knew there was nothing he could do for Reddy. He
couldn't dig a trench deep enough to protect a horse, so
it was only a question of time until he would go down as
the others had. The Indians were close now, driving in
from all sides. Again the tone of their yells changed. Now
it seemed to be one of savage hatred, as if the Indians
thought that by wiping out this band of white men they
could gain revenge for all the injuries that had been done
to their race over the centuries.

Other yells, too: the high screech of women and children
from the bluffs to the north, screams of encouragement
urging the braves on. The instant it was over and the whites

had been slaughtered, they would be down here with knives to slice and cut and mutilate.

Jedediah heard Forsyth's shouted command, "Hold your fire. Don't waste a bullet." And Beecher calling, "Get down, Colonel. For God's sake, get down."

Then Reddy was hit, a bullet smashing into his chest. Squealing, he lunged backward in his death agony, breaking the rope that held him to the willows. He went down on his knees, staggering up on his forelegs, and falling again, rolled over on his side. Jedediah cried out incoherently, wishing now, that the horse had been stolen with the other seven by the raiding party that had struck at dawn. He dropped his knife and plate, screaming a curse that was lost in the battle sounds.

Forsyth shouted, "Fire! Fire!"

Jedediah picked up his Spencer and crawled out of the hole. He laid the barrel of the rifle across Reddy's side, Harney moving up beside him. The first Indians coming in from the south were just breaking over the bank into the sandy stream bed. This was not an organized charge; some were riding singly, some in groups of three or four, and now when the tongues of flame lashed out from the muzzles of the Spencers, most of them turned back.

Jedediah fired at a single rider and saw him go off his horse in a great rolling fall. He emptied the Spencer and dropped behind the horse to reload, his hands trembling so that he was clumsy. Harney fired slowly and carefully, then he was back down beside Jedediah.

"The kid ain't much good when the squeeze got on," Harney said. "I figgered he'd be that way."

Jedediah glanced to his right. He hadn't noticed that Jamey was there, but now he saw the boy, cowering in a shallow trench, his face buried in the sand. He probably hadn't fired a shot, and Jedediah doubted that he would. He had known Jamey's inherent weakness, but he had expected something better than this.

"Damn you, Jamey!" he shouted. "Use your gun."

But the boy didn't stir. Maybe he hadn't heard. "No use," Harney said. "I've seen 'em go like that. He'll hate hisself the rest of his life, but he don't know it now."

His Spencer loaded, Jedediah raised up and slid the barrel over Reddy's side again. In the flat beyond the south bank an Indian had ridden into a buffalo wallow that was filled with water and his horse was mired down. Jedediah shot the warrior just as Harney yelled, "Watch out!" Another brave who had ridden across the island had come up from their rear. Jedediah dropped flat on his back as the Indian put his pony over Reddy in a great leap.

Staring upward, Jedediah saw the outflung legs of the pony, the long, graceful flow of his belly as the animal went on over, saw the wicked, painted face of the brave as he leaned sideways trying to bring his gun into line. Jedediah cringed, expecting to feel the slapping impact of the bullet, but the Indian, unable to swing the barrel down fast enough, didn't fire.

The pony hit the bank on the other side of Reddy, slid off into the sand, and floundered there until he recovered his balance. He went on, Jedediah too shaken for an instant to pick up his Spencer. When he did, the Indian was jumping the south bank of the stream. Jedediah emptied his rifle at the brave but apparently missed every shot.

He dropped back to reload, wondering why Harney hadn't brought the Indian down, then he saw that Harney was wounded and blood was pouring down his face. He was on his back, rolling his head back and forth on the ground and cursing as he yanked a rag out of his pocket and wiped the blood from his eyes.

"Let me look," Jedediah said.

"Go on, damn it!" Harney bellowed. "Give 'em hell afore they run us down."

But for the moment the seven-shot Spencers had eased the pressure. The Indians had suffered too many casualties to continue pressing the attack. In trying to carry off their dead and wounded, they had suffered more. The screams of encouragement from the bluffs to the north were now turning to cries of anguish. The Indians withdrew, the only firing coming from the sharpshooters hiding in the tall grass on both banks, and the answering shot from the scouts on the low end of the island.

From somewhere among the Indians a man yelled in good English, "There goes the last damn horse anyhow."

"Sounds like one of William Bent's renegade sons is out there," Harney said. "What are they doing?"

"Pulling out," Jedediah said. "You think we've whipped them?"

"Hell, no, we ain't whupped 'em." Harney dabbed at his forehead and cursed. "I can't see nothin'." He swore again, then he said, "We ain't seen Roman Nose. If he's with 'em, and I'll bet my bottom dollar he is, we'll have hell to pay yet."

In a lull in the firing, Jedediah heard Forsyth's voice. "Is there anyone here who can pray? We are beyond all human help, and if God does not help us there is none for us."

No one said anything, not even Andy Crowell. Jedediah crouching there behind the body of his horse, thought that Forsyth was a little late making his request. Jedediah had sensed the imminence of death for the last two days, and now he didn't have the slightest doubt that the Indians would overrun them and kill them, or capture them and hold them for torture; and that, he knew, would be far worse than death.

Chapter 14

JEDEDIAH had no concept of passing time. He was only aware of the sun being well up in the sky and cutting away the night chill.

Harney had tied the bandanna around his head and had stopped the flow of blood. With Jedediah, he dug the pit deeper until it gave both men adequate protection. Jamey, too, Jedediah noticed as he glanced at the boy, was taking advantage of the lull in the firing to deepen his trench.

"He won't fire a shot today," Harney said in disgust. "You'll see."

Word came that Forsyth was wounded twice in the leg, but he still had his voice and he used it to shout orders for the men to dig in deeper and to save their ammunition until they were sure they could make each bullet count. The Indian sharpshooters continued to keep up a sporadic fire. One of their bullets killed William Wilson, the first scout to die.

Jedediah heard someone near the center of the island yell, "If you fellows on the outside don't get up and shoot, them red bastards will be charging us again."

"The damned fool," Harney muttered. "Maybe he oughtta get out here and do a little shootin' hisself."

McCall and a scout who was with a man named Culver were apparently stung into action by the implied criticism. Both raised up to locate the Indians. Jedediah and Harney yelled, "Get down!" but their warning was too late. One of the sharpshooters shot Culver through the head and another wounded McCall in the neck.

Harney swore bitterly when he heard that Culver was dead. "A waste. A damned waste. Every man we lose cuts down our chance of rollin' 'em back the next time they hit us." He motioned toward the bluffs. "There's Roman Nose. I knowed he'd be in it. He's been waitin' till the dog soldiers got some o' the vinegar knocked out of 'em. Now they'll listen to him. He's got more fight savvy in his little finger than the rest of 'em put together have got in their heads."

Jedediah raised up briefly to see what was happening. Several hundred mounted warriors were milling around at the foot of the bluffs well out of rifle range. A big brave wearing a red sash around his waist was talking and gesticulating wildly, as if he was thoroughly angry at what had happened.

"It's my guess Roman Nose is givin' 'em hell for not grabbin' this island," Harney said. "Leastwise that's my guess. Trouble with Injuns is that they get so anxious to count coup and sech that they ain't much for follerin' orders. Even a scrapper like Roman Nose has a hell of a time gettin' 'em to do anything right."

"How many do you think there are?" Jedediah asked.

"Close to a thousand," Harney answered. "Hard to tell with so many of 'em hidin' in the grass and pot-shootin' any of us they get a bead on. I knowed we was chasin' a big party, but I ain't seen one Army man in ten you could tell anything to. Hell, we could of saved our hides yestiddy, but now we're in for it."

"Cheyennes?"

"Not all of 'em. Northern Cheyennes, all right, but there's some Oglalas and Brule Sioux, too. I ain't spotted no Arapahoes, but there's some with 'em—you can bet on it."

A bullet snapped over Jedediah's head and buried itself with a solid *thwack* into Reddy's body behind Jedediah. He dropped flat into the pit, then carefully raised his head so he had a partial view of the bluff through the grass. He was seeing something he didn't understand that bothered him. The mounted warriors were moving downstream around a bend in the creek. Jedediah could see no logical reason for such a move, but apparently the braves were following Roman Nose's orders, so there had to be a reason.

Suddenly a bugle sounded from among the Indians. Jedediah thought he had heard it earlier, but it had been during a period of heavy firing and he hadn't been sure. Now he was certain, for this blast came during a lull and there could be no mistaking the sound.

"What Indian would learn to blow a bugle?" Jedediah asked. "And where would they get one?"

"No trouble gettin' it," Harney said. "We ain't the first bunch that got nailed down and maybe wiped out. Just like they git most of their guns—off dead soldiers. But chances are it ain't no Injun blowin' it. Like I said while ago, William Bent's got some sons that've turned renegade. Could be one of 'em learned to toot a bugle at Fort Bent."

"They're ridin' downstream," Jedediah said. "Why?"

"Funny thing 'bout Injuns," Harney went on, as if he hadn't heard. "Take the Fetterman business a couple o' years ago. Red Cloud wiped 'em out. He's a general. Mebbe better'n Roman Nose. Either one of 'em could learn Phil Sheridan a trick or two. Right now Roman Nose is thinkin' he'll give us what Fetterman's command got."

Jedediah had been only half listening. He still could not understand the movement downstream around the bend; then a reasonable guess came to him. "Bill, you think Roman Nose is taking them downstream to organize them for a charge?"

"Downstream?" Harney shouted the word as if only then aware of what Jedediah had said. He sat bolt upright to see what was going on, then ducked back quickly just before a bullet whined above him where his head had been a moment before. "That'n damn near got me," he said as if it had been no more than an annoying flight of a wasp.

Jedediah glanced at the big man, unable to understand him. Yesterday he had talked openly about desertion. During the night he had actually tried to get away. Now he had the coolest head on the island. He was a realist, Jedediah decided, totally untouched by ambition or dreams of glory or a sense of responsibility to the others. Now that he was here, he would fight as hard as any man, and better than most.

"Can you snake yourself yonder to the Colonel?" Harney asked. "You're skinnier'n me. Besides, Brass Buttons wouldn't believe anything I said."

"Sure, but why should I?"

" 'Cause he needs to be told what they're up to. If we ain't ready for 'em, they'll run over us. You guessed it right. Purty soon you'll see 'em comin' around the bend like

69

they was right out o' hell, and we'd better be a shootin'."

"I'll tell him," Jedediah said.

He eased out of the pit and worked his way through the grass, not knowing how much time he had. He kept his body flat against the ground, propelling himself with his hands and toes. A burst of firing broke out from the foot of the island, then died. Young Jack Stillwell and two other men were down there in the tall grass. Jedediah felt better just knowing they were there. Stillwell and Louis Farley had the reputation of being the best shots in the command.

His progress seemed incredibly slow, but he hadn't been far from Forsyth's pit when he started. Now he called, "Colonel," and heard Forsyth's answer, "Over here." A moment later he crawled into the trench where Forsyth was lying. Beads of sweat were shiny on the officer's forehead. He was biting his lower lip against the agony of pain that racked his body.

The man was a soldier. Whatever mistakes of judgment he had made, he possessed the kind of courage around which legends are made. The thought occurred to Jedediah that if any of them survived, their stand on this island in the Dry Fork of the Republican would in time be the basis of a legend.

"Can't the doctor do anything for you?" Jedediah asked.

"Dr. Mooers is badly wounded in the head," Forsyth said. "I don't expect him to live until night. To make our plight worse, we left our medical supplies in camp. Of course it's impossible to go after them now. They'll be carried off by the Indians before we have a chance to get them."

Jedediah was silent for a moment, thinking that aside from Beecher and Forsyth they could not have lost a man they would miss more than the surgeon. Still, no one was to blame, for bullets in battle were never any respecter of rank. On the other hand, the loss of the medical supplies was unpardonable.

"You had something to tell me?" Forsyth asked.

"They've been drifting downstream around the bend," Jedediah said. "Harney and I made a guess that Roman Nose will lead a charge against us."

"You may be right," Forsyth said. "Well, if they run over us, they'll trample us or shoot us to death."

Forsyth hesitated, looking at Jedediah thoughtfully, then he said, "Go back to your trench, Jones. Beecher! McCall! Get ready to repel an attack. Have every man see that his rifle and revolver are fully loaded. Get the guns of the dead men and of the ones who are too severely wounded to shoot, and give them to the men on the lower end of the island."

Jedediah crawled out of the trench, momentarily exposing himself before the grass and weeds covered him. He felt as if his skin were a crawling thing covering his body, but no shot came. A moment later he was back in the pit with Harney.

"The doctor's badly wounded," Jedediah said, "and we left our medical supplies this morning."

Nothing seemed to surprise Harney. He said, "Cuts down our chances a little more, Jed. All we need to do now is to run out of ammunition."

Jedediah heard the shouted command, "Load up. Hold your fire until you're given the order."

"Here they come," Harney said. "By God, look at 'em! If I was somewhere else and could see this, I'd say it was a damned purty sight."

Jedediah agreed. He had never fully understood Indians. He doubted that any white man did, but he understood and admired courage. Here was a people fighting for their homes, and this, too, was something Jedediah could understand.

For a moment his heart quickened at the sight of this on-coming mass of horsemen, sixty wide and eight deep, Roman Nose in the front row. Then he thought of his dead sorrel, and he thought that they would kill him, too, if they could. He went cold and dead inside, his hands tightening on the Spencer. This was not the time to feel sympathy for the injured red men.

The Indians swept upstream, each painted warrior naked except for his moccasins and cartridge belt. They rode bare-back, their horse-hair ropes tied around the middle of their mounts in such a fashion that it went over their knees. They held their horses' manes with their left hands, their rifles above their heads in their right hands.

They stopped briefly just out of rifle range, the momen-tary silence creating a brittle pressure that was unbearable to Jedediah. The Indian sharpshooters in the grass had ceased firing; even the women and children watching from the bluffs had stopped screaming.

Once more Forsyth called, "Hold your fire until I give the order."

Roman Nose faced his men and spoke to them, motioned toward the island, then toward the women and children on

71

the cliff. He turned back toward the scouts and shook his fist at them. Tipping his head back and striking his mouth with his hand, he gave a war cry that must have been intended to call down aid from the Indian god of war. That was Jedediah's first thought, but whatever the cry was for, he knew he had never heard as spine-tingling a sound in his life.

They came at a gallop, each line perfect, but it was Roman Nose who held Jedediah's attention. He was a big man, six feet two or three, and certainly the most muscular Indian Jedediah had ever seen. He rode his chestnut horse with perfect balance. His war bonnet was a thing of beauty, two curved buffalo horns directly above his forehead, heron and eagle feathers streaming behind him in the wind.

Suddenly the sharpshooters opened up from the grass. "Keepin' us down," Harney said, "but they'll have to let up purty soon or they'll cut their own men down."

Harney was right. Just as the firing stopped, the bugle call came again, clear and sharp, and the encouraging screams of the watchers on the bluff rolled down to mingle with the war cries of the charging horde.

Jedediah, on his knees, saw that the men in front of him had turned to face the charge. He could not bring himself to look back at Jamey, for he knew the boy would be face down in the sand just as he had been earlier that morning during the first attack. He would live or die by what the others did, not by anything he did for himself.

"Now!" Forsyth shouted.

Beecher and McCall picked up the order. "Now!"

The sound of the volley was deafening as flame flashed out from the Spencers. The scouts' bullets tore great gaps in the front rows of the Indians as men and horses went down. They closed ranks and came on, Roman Nose untouched and still in the first row. He held his heavy rifle over his head, yelling his war cry as if certain his medicine was good this day.

Another volley and another, and a fourth. A medicine man out on the left flank fell from his horse, and for a moment Jedediah thought the charge was broken, but he was wrong. Once more the Indians closed ranks, the prairie behind them sprinkled with dead and dying men and horses. Still they came on, almost to the island now. A fifth volley, and then the sixth, and Roman Nose went off his horse, the medicine that had kept him alive through so many fights failing him now.

Roman Nose was the key man in the charge, the nerve center of its courage. The instant he fell, the attack stopped as if it had hit an invisible wall. Another volley took its toll, but the Indians, even in the face of that deadly fire, picked up Roman Nose's body and carried him to safety.

The scouts were on their feet, cheering and yelling, their revolvers bucking in their hands as they emptied them at the fleeing Indians. A handful of warriors had reached the foot of the island before the attack failed. If they had come on, and they would have if Roman Nose had not fallen, they would have overrun the island and trampled the scouts to death as Roman Nose must have planned.

Now the main body of Indians divided and raced away from the island in a desperate effort to escape the revolver fire. A moment before there had been tight organization and great courage; now there was only demoralization and panic.

Jedediah was amazed to find himself on his feet cheering with the rest of them, his smoking revolver in his hand. He was part of the group; he was involved as he had never been involved in anything before. Suddenly a great rush of pride swept over him as it must have with every man who was on his feet, pride at snatching life from death, victory from what had been certain defeat, pride at having enough self-control to stand and fight in front of the flying hoofs of five-hundred horsemen.

"Get down!" Forsyth shouted. "Lie down!"

McCall picked up the command, "Get down, damn it! You want your heads blown off?"

Harney grabbed Jedediah by an arm and yanked him into the pit. The others dropped into their trenches just as the sharpshooters opened up from the grass and raked the island with a vicious fire. Again the screams from the bluff changed to shrieks of grief. The women had been certain of victory, Jedediah thought as he reloaded his guns, but they had seen the charge collapse, many of their sons and husbands killed or wounded.

From that distance none of the squaws could tell who had suffered the loss of their loved ones. If their screams proved anything at all, Jedediah told himself, it proved that Indians had the same human emotions the whites did, that being primitive or civilized had little to do with the way a person felt about the insanity of war and the violent death of those who were loved.

He lay on his back and stared at the sky, the hot sun

73

pounding at him. Powder smoke drifted across the island; the smell of it lingered in his nostrils. He could see and he could smell; he was alive. God willing, he might still stand in front of Cally Moore someday and tell her he had come back to her.

Chapter 15

JEDEDIAH saw Lieutenant Beecher rise from his rifle pit and stagger to Forsyth's trench and drop into it. At the moment there was no firing, and in this lull Jedediah heard Beecher say that he had received his death wound. Forsyth said something that did not reach Jedediah, Beecher said something back; after that there was no more talk between the two.

Harney, too, heard what Beecher said. He swore and shook his head at Jedediah. "Now, ain't that a hell of a note? The only Army officer we've got who knows anything about Injun fighting gets kilt, and the other one who don't know nuthin' 'bout it gets plugged but he goes right on givin' orders."

"We've got to have somebody giving orders," Jedediah said.

"Yeah, I reckon," Harney agreed reluctantly. "We'd sure have a scatteration if we didn't."

For a time Jedediah still lay staring at the sky, the sun moving toward high noon, the day growing hotter with each passing minute. He could not keep from thinking about Fred Beecher. He had not known the Lieutenant well—just enough to realize that here was a man he would have liked to know better. He was, by any standard Jedediah could think of, a soldier and gentleman, and to Fred Beecher that would have been the greatest of compliments.

Jedediah knew something about the Beechers—Harriet Beecher Stowe the author, and Henry Ward Beecher the minister—and he knew how deeply they had been involved in the Abolitionist movement. Now the bitter irony of it struck him, that the Beecher family, which had done so much to give equality to the Negro, would have one of its members killed in a fight with another minority race which was struggling for survival. Fred Beecher had fought heroically up to the moment he had been shot, but Jedediah was convinced that in his heart the Lieutenant had a great sympathy for the Indians.

"Are they right, Bill?" Jedediah called out. "The Indians, I mean?"

"Sure they're right," Harney said. "Any man is right who fights for his home and his family and his way o' livin'. You'd fight for it, too, wouldn't you, Jed?"

"Sure I would, but that's not the question. If they're right, why are we fighting them?"

" 'Cause they'll kill us if we don't," Harney answered. "I guess none of us want to die, less'n it's Redig. We're right, too, if it makes any difference, which it sure as hell don't. Everybody figgers he's right or he wouldn't be fightin'."

"I guess so," Jedediah said, but he wasn't satisfied with the answer.

"Take in the war," Harney went on. "The Yanks figgered they was right. So did the Johnny Rebs. They both prayed for God to help 'em. Now didn't that put God in a squeeze?" He laughed sourly. "When I first knowed the Injuns as a boy, they wanted to get along with the whites—most of 'em anyway. But it didn't take 'em long to learn they couldn't trust us bastards. Take that son-of-a-bitch of a Chivington. He murders a lot of women and children at Sand Creek and raises hell for years afterwards. It's a battle, the newspapers say. But when the whites get kilt like they done under Fetterman, it's a massacree."

He snorted in disgust. For the first time since Jedediah had met him, Harney was dead serious. He went on, "The only thing I'm interested in is savin' my hair. When you get down to cases, nuthin' else counts with any of us, 'cept mebbe Redig, and he's got something wrong with him. We may have a hard time livin', but we hate like hell to quit. So-o-o, if we ain't gonna quit, we'd better kill us a passel o' Injuns."

Harney was right. Every time Jedediah looked at his dead sorrel, a great burst of anger burned through his body like an outpouring of molten lava. He would kill all the Indians he could if that was what it took to survive. He wanted to live now more than he had ever wanted to in his life; he wanted to go back to Cally and tell her that he loved her, and that he had been wrong.

If he had learned anything at all since he had left Fort Hays, he had learned that. He had been cursed with a talent for seeing both sides of an issue. Now he saw the other side of this one; and even when he looked at Reddy, he could not entirely wipe the Indians' side from his mind.

Matthew Redig crawled to the edge of their pit and stared down at them. His broad body trembled with excitement, his face that had been so expressionless was bright and eager. He said, "I killed five of the bastards. You hear me? I killed five of them. I know I did because I saw them fall."

"That's good shootin'." Harney glanced at Jedediah, puzzled, and turned his gaze back to Redig. "Yep, right good shootin!"

"You kill some, Jones?" Redig demanded.

"Yes."

"What about you, Harney?" Redig asked suspiciously.

"Sure, I got me a few."

The man acted as if he hadn't heard. He stared past Jedediah and Harney trying to see who was in the next pit. "Who's yonder?" he asked. "On the other side of you?"

"Jamey Burns," Jedediah said, suddenly realizing that Redig, half crazy as he was, might kill Jamey if he knew how the boy had performed.

"What about him?" Redig demanded. "He kill some?"

"I wasn't watching," Jedediah said. "You'd better get back to your trench. If they hit us again, you'll want to be where you can kill some more."

"You sure would," Harney said quickly. "They'll come again, too, Redig. You can count on it."

Redig considered it a moment, frowning as if his mind was slow to grasp even this simple suggestion, then he nodded and crawled through the grass to his trench. Harney looked at Jedediah. "You see what I seen? He's as crazy as if he'd been eatin' loco weed. I knowed it when he tackled me yestiddy, but I didn't figger he was this bad."

"Bad, all right," Jedediah agreed. "I'm going to see Jamey."

"Wastin' your time," Harney said.

Jedediah knew he was, but he had to try. He was surprised when he realized this was so, but he was being surprised many times about himself now. He had little faith in the future—the odds were too great. If the Indians did not charge again, but simply settled down to a siege, time would win for them. Two scouts were dead. The surgeon and Beecher were dying. Others had been wounded.

No, there was little chance of surviving, but whether he did or not, he was a different man from what he had been even twenty-four hours ago. He could see Cally's face clearly in his mind; he could hear her voice quoting John Donne, "No man is an island, entire of itself." Now he knew what Donne had meant when he'd penned those words, but what surprised him the most was the fact that Cally had intuitively sensed the truth of Donne's writings.

When he reached Jamey's pit, he saw that the hole was deeper than it needed to be, and that the boy was frantically trying to dig it still deeper. He said, "Jamey, you'd better do some shooting the next time they come."

The boy rolled over on his back to stare at Jedediah. His hands trembled; the left corner of his mouth twitched at regular intervals as if it were a pulse beat controlled by the hammering of his heart. His staring eyes were startlingly red against the paper-white skin of his face.

"I can't, Mr. Jones." The boy swallowed, and then he said defiantly, "You shouldn't have let me come. I don't belong here."

"Let you come?" Jedediah started to curse the kid, then caught himself. He understood Jamey, and realized that he was to be pitied. "I guess you've forgotten that I did all I could to keep you from coming. Now I'll tell you something you'd better know. I kept Matthew Redig from asking you how many Indians you killed. If he finds out the kind of coward you've been, he'll cut your guts out."

Jamey's body went slack. He flung an arm over his face and left it there, and Jedediah saw that he was crying.

Jedediah crawled back to his pit and shook his head at Harney. "You're right. I remember a quotation from Sophocles: 'Death is not the greatest of ills; it is worse to want to die and not be able to.'" He thought about the words a moment, then added, "I don't suppose Jamey knows he wants to die, but I think he does. He'd be better off. At least he'd be at peace."

"Like I told you," Harney said indifferently, "he'll hate hisself the rest of his life, but you can't do nuthin' for him. He can't do nuthin' for hisself, either, far as that goes."

A burst of firing came from the Indian sharpshooters. Some of the scouts answered, but it was blind firing, a waste of bullets which neither Forsyth nor McCall encouraged. Jedediah could not see any Indians near the island, just the mounted men at the base of the bluffs to the north. They were milling around in confusion, showing the aimless condition in which Roman Nose's death had left them. If there were any sharpshooters in the grass along the south bank,

Jedediah could not see them, and he knew it would be certain death to stand up for a better look.

A scout named Burke, in the middle of the island, had dug his trench deep enough to find water. When Jedediah heard what had happened, he crawled through the grass to the pit that was now a shallow well and filled his canteen. The water was muddy, but at least it eased the tightness of his parched throat.

He filled Harney's canteen and took it back to him, then returned to help move the wounded to the center of the island, a slow and difficult task. No one dared show his body above the grass and brush, for the sharpshooters were sniping steadily at the scouts. When Andy Crowell hoisted his hat on a willow stick, it was immediately riddled with bullets.

Crowell grinned weakly at Jedediah. "Keep your head out of your hat if you show it, Slim."

"That's good advice," Jedediah agreed.

He wondered if Crowell had saved any souls today. He was tempted to ask, for if the men were ever to be of a mind to listen to him, it would be now, but he could not bring himself to put the question into words. He sensed that during these last frightful hours Andy Crowell had forgotten his purpose in coming, and he remembered that when Forsyth had asked someone to pray, Crowell had remained silent.

The sun was well past the point of high noon when Sharp Grover called from the low end of the island, "They're fixin' to make another run at us, Colonel."

Jedediah crawled back to his pit as Forsyth called, "Load up. Get ready to repel a charge."

When Jedediah reached Harney, he found the man as cheerful as ever. "This one won't amount to a damn. They lost their appetite for runnin' over us when Roman Nose's medicine turned bad. They'll make a try, but their hearts will fail 'em."

Jedediah picked up his Spencer, wishing he could be as sure. Even if they beat off this attack, and the next, and the next, what hope was there? The horses were dead. They were a hundred miles from Fort Wallace, perhaps more. Even if the Indians withdrew, the scouts would never reach the fort, burdened by their wounded as they were.

Holding his Spencer as he crouched in the pit and waited, Jedediah wondered about the thoughts that were in Forsyth's mind now.

Chapter 16

THE Indians made the charge at about two o'clock that afternoon. Watching from his rifle pit, Jedediah saw a war chief in the middle of the first rank, slightly ahead of the others and gesturing with his right hand for the braves behind him to keep coming. Whoever he was, he failed to give the inspiring leadership that Roman Nose had demonstrated in the desperate charge of the morning.

"Who's leading them this time?" Jedediah asked.

"Dunno," Harney said. "Could be Dull Knife if he's with them, but I dunno if he is or not."

Jedediah had a feeling the Indians were making this charge because they felt they had to, not because they seriously intended to overrun the island as they certainly had planned to do that morning. For some reason he was reminded of a watch with the main spring gone.

Stillwell and the two men with him in the grass at the low end of the island did not wait for the order to fire. As soon as the Indians were within rifle range the three scouts opened up, knocking one warrior off his horse. That was the end of the charge.

The Indians divided into two lines, making Jedediah think of a river current striking a great rock. One line rode along the south side of the island, the other on the north, both swinging wide and keeping well out of range. The Indians yelled and gestured as if taunting the scouts to get out of their rifle pits and fight. Eventually they gathered again at the foot of the bluffs where they milled around in confusion as they had done earlier in the afternoon.

When Matthew Redig realized that the Indians were not making a serious fight of it, he jumped up on the lip of his rifle pit and shook his fist at them. He yelled, "Come on, you sons-of-bitches. Come in closer so I can get a shot at you."

"Get down, Redig," McCall shouted. "You trying to commit suicide?"

Andy Crowell leaped out of his pit, grabbed Redig by the legs, and brought him down. Crowell said, loudly and angrily, "After this is over, you can shoot yourself if that's what you're trying to get done, but right now we need your rifle."

From where he crouched in his trench, Jedediah could not hear what Redig said. A moment later he saw Crowell crawl back into his own pit. Several Indian snipers had fired at Redig when he was on his feet, but apparently he had not been hit.

As far as Jedediah knew, Matthew Redig had never told anyone about his past, or his reason for joining the column. Whatever it was, Jedediah thought, the man must have been driven by some terrible and compelling memory to seek death.

Jedediah was reminded once more of the quotation from Sophocles, and the irony of what had happened struck him. Jamey Burns, who was of no value to himself or anyone else, was alive. Matthew Redig, who apparently didn't care whether he lived or died, was alive. But Wilson and Culver, who had wanted to live, were dead. Dr. Mooers and Fred Beecher were dying, and Beecher, particularly, had faced a bright future.

Harney lay on his back in the bottom of the pit, his sweat-stained hat pulled over his eyes, the Spencer beside him. He said, "It's like I told you. They didn't really aim to make that one stick."

"Will they try again?" Jedediah asked.

"Mebbe, but they'll never make another run like they done this mornin'. Chances are they'll throw a ring around the island so we can't get away, then they'll wait for us to starve or try walkin' through 'em."

"We don't have a chance. Is that what you're saying?"

"No, I ain't sayin' that at all. Injuns act like kids sometimes. They'll fight like hell, then the chiefs git to jawin' and won't take orders from nobody, or they start thinkin' o' something else they want to do or see and off they go." He was silent a moment, then he added, "I figger they'll stick here for a spell. Losin' Roman Nose has made 'em mad."

"We might be relieved by a column from Fort Wallace," Jedediah said.

"Sure, and we might get rescued by a band of angels from Heaven," Harney said. "Just one thing—nobody at Fort Wallace knows where we are. Forsyth didn't know hisself till he hit that hot trail. Supposin' Bankhead sends out a column? They wouldn't find us. This is a hell of a big country, Jed."

Jedediah was silent, knowing that what Harney said was true. The big man rattled on, "I seen Roman Nose a few times. At a guess I'd say he was about thirty. He was a Southern Cheyenne, but he'd throwed in with the Northern Cheyennes. His real name was Sauts, meanin' The Bat. After he got older, that damned nose o' his just naturally took his face over. Looked like a beak of an old, mean hawk. Some white started calling him Roman Nose, and now his own people call him Waquini. It means Hook Nose.

"I've met a passel o' Indians I liked. Dull Knife for one. Black Kettle for another, but I figgered Roman Nose for a son-of-a-bitch right from the first. He had the thinnest lips I ever seen. When he'd screw 'em up in a grin and look at you, you could figger he was thinkin' how your scalp would look hangin' in his lodge, and by God, he had a pile of 'em."

Jedediah had been only half listening. Now he said, "Forsyth will send somebody for help. There's a chance of getting through, isn't there?"

Harney took his hat off his face and sat up, his gaze on Jedediah. "Yeah," he said finally, "there's a chance, just like there is that Bankhead will send some of his boys huntin' for us and they'll find us. 'Bout one in a million, I'd say. Meanwhile we'll sit here eatin' horse meat till it rots. We'll probably be eatin' it afterwards, too."

"Horse meat!" Jedediah looked at Reddy, the idea of eating the sorrel that had carried him for years over so many miles utterly repellent to him. "If anybody cuts into Reddy, I'll kill him. I'm no cannibal."

"Well, now, that's a right interestin' notion, Jed." Harney laughed softly. "You're sayin' that horses are people. In some ways I reckon they're better'n people, but the point is that when you're starvin', you'll eat anything, includin' people. I have. Man meat ain't so bad when you get over the idea that it's the wrong thing to eat. When you get hungry enough, you get over it, all right. Fact is, a man gets over all his kid notions of what's right and wrong when he's desperate. You wind up knowin' you ain't no more civilized than the Injun you're sayin' is a savage."

Jedediah turned away from Harney, shocked in spite of himself. A sudden and terrifying thought hit him. Harney would kill him and eat him if they were still alive after the horse meat was gone.

Harney smiled as if pleased by the disturbance he had raised in Jedediah's mind. He said, "I reckon we can't build no fires yet, but I've et plenty of raw meat in my day, and right now I'm hungry."

Jedediah faced him. "Bill, if you touch Reddy—"

"Cool down, Jed," Harney interrupted. "I got my own horse to eat. I tell you what. We'll share him. It sure would upset your stummick if you had to eat that sorrel o' yours."

Harney picked up his butcher knife, ran it across his pants leg to clean it, then crawled to where his horse lay, close to Reddy. He cut a long strip of meat from a ham and crawled back chewing on it, the blood dribbling down into his salt-and-pepper beard. Jedediah stared at him for a moment, then a wave of nausea hit him and he gagged, but there was nothing in his stomach to come up except the muddy water he had drunk from Burke's shallow well.

He crawled out of the pit and through the grass toward the center of the island. He had known a good deal about Harney's background, but he had not realized until now how much of an animal the man was. He was sure of one thing. If any of them survived, it would be Braggin' Bill Harney. Then he was shocked by the thought that, in time, and if he became hungry enough, he might do the very thing that had made him mentally term Harney an animal.

He spent the rest of the afternoon helping Andy Crowell and a few others with the wounded. There was little they could do without medical supplies except lift the heads of the injured men and hold a canteen to their lips, or soak a rag in water and place it on a man's forehead. The day remained hot, and late in the afternoon many of the wounded were feverish.

Beecher and Dr. Mooers were still alive, but Jedediah held no hope for either man. Now and then Beecher cried out in delirium, and once the words "My poor mother" came clearly to Jedediah's ears. Mooers remained in a stupor, but he must have been partially conscious at times, for he occasionally reached out to touch Forsyth as if to assure himself that his commander was still there.

Jedediah was not sure that even Forsyth would survive. He had a scalp wound which gave him a good deal of pain, he had a bullet in his right thigh, and his left leg was broken below the knee, but in spite of his wounds, he left no doubt about who was in command.

At intervals McCall or Grover crawled through the grass to talk to Forsyth, and then returned to his rifle pit. Forsyth insisted on knowing what was going on. The Indian sharp-shooters still fired sporadically, just often enough to let the scouts know they were still out there in the grass and that if anyone showed himself, he would get what Culver and Wilson had.

In order to keep Forsyth informed, Jedediah lifted his head occasionally and dropped it immediately, catching a brief glimpse of the bluff and the Indians along the base. Once he crawled to the north bank of the island and lay on his belly for several minutes, staring through the fringe of grass at the milling Indians.

Presently he became aware that the mounted warriors were drifting downstream again. Another charge! He wondered if Harney's optimistic prophecy would be proved right again. But there was one big difference from the charge that morning, perhaps a fatal one. When Roman Nose had led the attack, nearly every scout had been able to fire his rifle. Now two were dead, two more were dying, and many were wounded, some slightly, but others too severely to make any effort to defend themselves.

Jedediah crawled back through the grass and told Forsyth what he had seen. Forsyth groaned. "Then we'll have to do it again. I think we can. Get back to your pit." He raised his voice. "McCall. Grover. See that the men are ready to repel another charge."

Jedediah wormed his way to his and Harney's trench, wondering if his partner would still be eating raw horse meat. He wasn't. Even his beard was reasonably free of dried blood.

Harney grinned when he saw Jedediah. He said, "You got hungry, didn't you?"

"No," Jedediah said. "They're coming at us again."

"Well, nothing like a full stummick to help a man draw a true bead," Harney said.

It was a nightmare, Jedediah thought, and he wondered if death was the only means of freeing himself from it.

Chapter 17

DARK clouds had swept across the sky, covering the sun and lowering the temperature by at least twenty degrees. It was about six now, Jedediah judged. He rubbed a hand across his sweaty, stubbled-covered face. A rain was coming. The night would be a cold one again, but at the moment the prospect seemed pleasant after the heat of the day.

"Here they come," Harney said. "They're doing a little better'n they done this afternoon." He glanced at Jedediah and winked. "Tell you what, Jed. I'll bet my horse against yours that this is the last charge they'll make."

"No."

Harney laughed softly. "Well, I reckon there's plenty o' meat on my hoss. He was a damned poor excuse when it came to travelin', but he eats purty good."

Jedediah wasn't listening. He was watching the Indians come up the valley at a gallop. Apparently they had recruited more men, for in spite of their losses, this group looked as large as the one that had attacked under Roman Nose. If anything they seemed to be in a greater frenzy than they had been that morning. Some were firing rifles, others were using bows and arrows, and all were screaming their war cries, that to Jedediah was still the most terrifying sound he had ever heard.

For him, the morning attack had been a sort of magnificent pageant, but he didn't have that feeling now. There was a nightmarish quality about this charge, as if he had lived this moment before, a feeling that it would be repeated again and again until the scouts' ammunition was gone and the next charge would be the last.

Stillwell and the men with him squeezed off their shots before Forsyth gave the order, then Jedediah heard the shouted command, "Fire!" Every scout who was physically able, except Jamey Burns, was on his knees in his rifle pit. The flash of powder flame danced from the muzzles of the Spencers, the volley making a tremendous crashing sound that momentarily deafened Jedediah.

The front line of the Indians was chewed to pieces. The

second and third volleys were almost a waste of ammunition. One brave came on to reach the foot of the island before young Stillwell brought him down; the rest broke and ran. Once out of rifle range, they contented themselves by yelling and taunting the scouts with obscene gestures that brought a laugh from Harney.

"It's the damnedest thing," Harney said. "Look at 'em. Their hearts failed 'em again and they're ashamed of theirselves, so they try to make up for it by telling us we're cowards." He glanced at Jedediah. "Well, good thing you didn't take my bet or you'd have lost your hoss."

"Tomorrow's still coming," Jedediah said.

"Sure, but they're finished. They'll pop away at us from the grass and they'll keep a purty tight circle around us so we won't walk through 'em tonight, but looks like they've finally got it through their heads that they ain't gonna run over us. They won't find another Roman Nose right away. You know, that bastard hadn't ever been whupped and he didn't figger he would be. Wonder what went wrong with his medicine?"

Jedediah glanced at him, suddenly realizing that Harney had lived with Indians a long time, so long that maybe he actually believed in the intangible thing they called "medicine." Perhaps he carried around his neck a buckskin pouch which held a secret ingredient that he used in his medicine, as all Indians did. The man was more savage than civilized, more Indian than white, or so it seemed, but the part that Jedediah found most puzzling was the fact that Harney had picked him as his partner. He sensed that if Harney survived, he would see to it that Jedediah survived, too.

McCall reached them then, relaying Forsyth's orders: "Yank your saddle off your horse and use the saddles to improve your rifle pits. Dig a trench between your pit and the next one so that we can communicate with each other without crawling through the grass. When that's done, cut meat off your horse and bury it in the sand so it won't rot so fast. We may be here a long time. Jones, the Colonel wants you."

McCall went on to Jamey's trench and lay for a moment on his stomach, staring down at the boy in contempt. Finally he said, "You stinking, yellow-bellied son-of-a-bitch! You heard the order. Now get busy or I'll come down there and cut your heart out."

"Yes, sir." Jamey swallowed, and repeated, "Yes, sir."

Forsyth and McCall didn't miss much, Jedediah thought

as he crawled through the grass to Forsyth's trench. He hadn't been sure that in the excitement of the attacks they had known about Jamey, but they had. Sooner or later everyone in the command would know, and the boy would be a pariah among them.

Jedediah slid into Forsyth's pit, saying, "McCall told me you wanted to see me."

Forsyth studied him for a moment, his face clearly showing the agony he was suffering from his wounds. He said, "We'll have to try to get a man through their lines after it gets dark. The question is who to send. Do you think Harney would try it?"

Jedediah considered it a moment, recalling how Harney had wanted to leave yesterday, and later had tried to sneak away during the night. He had a stubborn and vindictive streak in him; the knowledge that Forsyth wanted him to go was probably enough to make him refuse. Finally Jedediah said, "I don't think he will."

"I didn't think he would," Forsyth said. "It's too bad. With the exception of young Stillwell and Grover, he's the best-equipped man here."

"I'll try it," Jedediah said.

"No, a shorter man would have a better chance," Forsyth said. "Whoever goes will have to travel at night and hide during the day. A man as tall as you will have trouble finding a place to hide. Besides, you can do more with young Burns than anyone else. I've seen too many men like him. Under the right circumstances he could be a danger to all of us."

McCall joined them then, and Forsyth went on, "Jones, tell Harney to come here. Sergeant, I want to see Stillwell, Grover, Pliley, Trudeau, Whitney, and Donovan. Anyone else you think would be willing to try to get through to Wallace."

"Yes, sir," McCall said, and disappeared in the grass.

Jedediah hesitated, convinced that it was a mistake to ask Harney. He said, "I don't think Harney will do it."

"You've told me that, but I'm still going to ask him," Forsyth snapped. "I suppose you're wondering why I sent for you and then do not do what you advise. I hoped your answer would be different. In any case, I have to ask him. You might be mistaken."

"He's stubborn," Jedediah said. "If you order him—"

"I won't order him. I'll ask him to volunteer." When Jedediah still didn't move, Forsyth raised his voice, "Damn it, you said you belonged to the Colorado Volunteers during the war. You were at Glorieta. Didn't they teach you to obey orders?"

"Yes, sir," Jedediah said, and slipped out of the trench and wormed his way to his and Harney's pit.

He found Harney industriously cutting slices of meat from his horse and burying them in the sand. Jedediah looked at Reddy's stiff body and felt his throat tighten. Maybe he was foolish to refuse to let the animal be cut up. He realized that it was not a rational decision, that his emotions were ruling him, stupidly so perhaps, yet at this moment he would not have had it any other way.

"I figgered it was more important to take care o' this meat than it was to dig more trenches." Harney gave Jedediah a sharp look. "Get some special orders from the Colonel? Takin' McCall's place mebbe?"

Jedediah shook his head. "The Colonel wants to see you. He sent McCall after some others."

Harney gave his knife a swipe across his pants leg, his shrewd eyes fixed on Jedediah's face. "Pickin' his men to go for help. That it?"

"That's right."

"Well, sir, if Colonel Brass Buttons thinks I'm gonna walk a hundred miles through the damned Cheyennes, he can think again."

"What difference does it make?" Jedediah asked. "If nobody goes, we all die. You might as well die out there as here."

"Yeah," Harney said agreeably. "That kind o' makes sense, but you're forgettin' I wanted to go yestiddy. Last night I tried to get away when we had hosses and I could of made it, but by God, you was gonna shoot me. Now I ain't leavin' the island. I told you that you'd wish you'd let me go."

"All right, I wasn't sent here to argue with you," Jedediah said wearily. "Go see Forsyth. I guess you can do that."

Harney raised a hand to the blood-stained bandage around his head, reminding Jedediah that he had been wounded. Perhaps it was hurting him worse than Jedediah realized, but it didn't make any difference—he wouldn't have gone for help anyway.

"Sure, I guess I can go see Colonel Brass Buttons," Harney said, and driving his knife into the sand up to the handle, crawled out of the pit.

The first drops of rain came then. Jedediah tipped his

head and felt the cool moisture on his face; he held his hands out, palm up. The light was very thin, the sky dark and forbidding. Was there any hope, any hope at all? Could they hold out until help came? Or would help ever come?

He licked his lips and rubbed his face with his hands. He thought of what Harney had said. One chance in a million! As he crawled out of the pit and followed Harney, he thought that no sane man would ever gamble on odds like that.

Chapter 18

BY THE time Jedediah reached Forsyth's trench, the light had become so faint that the Indian sharpshooters could not distinguish anything on the island. Apparently they had withdrawn. At least, there had been no firing from them for some time. The men Forsyth had sent for were standing around his trench looking down at him, feeling that it was safe to remain upright.

"You all know that someone has to get through to Fort Wallace or we'll die right here," Forsyth said. "If help doesn't reach us, either the Indians or starvation will kill us. I have a field map and a compass I'll give to the man who goes. By my calculations we're a little better than a hundred miles from Wallace, maybe a hundred and ten. I believe we can hold out for six days. A man should get to Fort Wallace and a relief column reach us in that time."

"You're overlooking something, Colonel," Sharp Grover said. "The Indians have lost a lot of men today and they're mad. It's kind o' like tipping a beehive over. They'll be so thick round this island tonight that a snake can't get through."

"Somebody's got to try, Grover," Forsyth said. "It's a simple question of whether we die here together, or whether one of you will get through and give us a chance."

"It's sure death to try," Grover said sullenly. "Nobody can make it."

"Do you have a better suggestion?" Forsyth asked.

"Chances are Bankhead has sent a relief column out to

look for us before now," Grover said. "I figger it's safer to wait here."

"He'll wait a week before he sends anybody out," Forsyth said, "and even then they wouldn't find us for another week. We can't last that long."

A moment of silence, a cold drizzle of rain falling on them, then Harney said slowly, "I figger a man can get through, Colonel. I've wiggled through Indian lines more'n once. Sure, they'll be lookin' for us, mebbe countin' on all of us makin' a run downstream afore mornin', but I still say a man can make it with a leetle luck."

"Will you try it?" Forsyth asked.

Jedediah sensed that this was the question Harney was waiting for, that he sought an opportunity to turn Forsyth down.

"No, sir, I won't," Harney said. "I knowed yestiddy what we was ridin' into and I done my damnedest to get us turned back. If you don't know what happened, Colonel, I'll tell you. Redig tried to knife me. You gave me a tongue blisterin'. McCall was fixin' to shoot me. Last night I tried to sneak out o' camp. I was aimin' to head for Wallace. Wouldn't have been no trick to it on a hoss, but the guard shoved his rifle into me and says to git back to camp. I figger I done all I could. Now, by God, I'm stayin' right here."

"If you tried to run last night without orders," Forsyth said, "you should have been reported to me. Who was the guard?"

"And git him shot?" Harney laughed shortly. "Funny thing, Colonel, but I disremember who he was, come to think of it. But Grover here—he's the guide. He's supposed to know the country. Looks to me like it's up to him to make this here sashay."

Silence again, Jedediah beginning to understand some of Harney's reasons for being bitter. He had applied for the job of guide and had been turned down. Instead, Forsyth had hired Sharp Grover, and Harney had not considered Grover competent from the first. "He knows the Sioux, all right, but he sure don't know nuthin' 'bout Cheyennes," Harney had told Jedediah when he'd heard who had been picked. So, because of professional jealousy and injured pride, Harney would stay on the island and die with the rest of the command rather than try to reach the fort. Not a rational decision, but it was Braggin' Bill Harney's way.

Grover remained sullenly silent. Finally it was young Jack Stillwell who said, "I'll go if someone will go with me."

Again the silence ribboned out painfully until Pierre Trudeau said reluctantly, "I'll try it."

"Good!" Forsyth said, pleased. "I think you'd better wait until about midnight. The relief party will have to bring ambulances, because a good many of us can't walk or ride. That presents the question of whether ambulances can be brought directly here from the fort. What do you think, Grover?"

"No," he said quickly. "The country's too rough. They'll have to swing north until they reach the Republican, and then follow it."

"All right, Stillwell," Forsyth said. "Tell that to Colonel Bankhead."

"He's wrong again," Harney said. "Colonel, it'll waste a hell of a lot of time to swing around and come up the Republican. I know the country between here and Wallace. It's not too rough for wagons. If they're gonna get here in time to save our hides, they'd better come the shortest way they can."

"I have to take the word of my guide," Forsyth said sharply.

"Sure, you do that," Harney said amiably, "but don't figger on no relief party getting here in six days. I got a notion or two for Stillwell and Trudeau. Want to hear 'em, or are all the notions supposed to come from your guide?"

"We'll listen," Forsyth said.

"Well, sir, if I was goin', I'd take off my boots. I'd walk backwards for a spell, too. Come mornin', if some Injuns pick up the tracks, mebbe they'll think it's one o' their'n. A sock foot makes a track kind o' like a moccasin. If they don't figger someone got through, they won't be huntin' for 'em. That'll give Stillwell and Trudeau a hell of a lot better chance. They ain't goin' far the first night nohow."

"That's a good idea, Colonel," Stillwell said. "If the Indians pick up our boot tracks, they'll come right to us, no matter how good a place we find to hide."

"Use whatever stratagems you need to use," Forsyth said. "That's up to you, of course. When you reach Wallace, give Colonel Bankhead a complete account of our condition. Tell him that nearly half of my command is dead or wounded."

"I'll tell him," Stillwell said.

When the others had gone, Jedediah said, "I'd like permission to leave the island after it's dark. It occurs to me that I might find some things we need. A shovel anyway."

"Permission granted," Forsyth said; "but you'd better wait until Stillwell and Trudeau leave. And be careful. Indians will be skulking around the island all night. They won't attack, but if you stumble onto some of them, you'll have the fight of your life."

"I'll watch for them," Jedediah said, and returned to his rifle pit, where Harney had resumed cutting horse meat.

"Damned fools," Harney said bitterly. "If I'd been guide, we'd never have got into this hole."

"Forsyth had made up his mind he wasn't going back without having an Indian fight," Jedediah said. "I don't think you or anybody else could have stopped him."

"Mebbe not." Harney dug his knife fiercely into the horse's ham, then said again, "Damned fools."

Jedediah drew his diary from his pocket and, bending forward to shield the book from the rain, began to write.

> *On an island in the stream bed*
> *of the Dry Fork of the Republican,*
> *Sept. 17, 1868*

We are surrounded and pinned down on this island. During the day we have been attacked repeatedly and have beaten them back. Harney says they will not charge us again, but starvation looms ahead as a greater danger than Indians. Two men will leave at midnight to go for help. Whatever hope we have of living depends upon them.

He lifted his pencil from the paper, thinking of other things he wanted to say, about Harney and Jamey Burns and Matthew Redig, and yes, about Forsyth, too, how his ambition had overpowered his judgment until he had brought them all to this place. Now their future seemed utterly hopeless.

His thoughts turned bitter. It would not do anyone the slightest bit of good to read what he thought about these men if he died here on this piece of sand. On the other hand, if by some miracle he lived, he would put down later what he remembered, and by then time would strain some of the bitterness from his memory.

He replaced his pencil and diary in his pocket, noticing that tiny points of light on the bluff were visible through the drizzle. The Indians had built fires, a luxury the scouts could not afford. The death chant and lamentations of the squaws seemed to grow in volume as the light failed. It would go on all night, he thought, making sleep difficult, if not impossible. The braves would slip close to the island to remove the bodies of their dead and wounded. As Forsyth had said, there was a good possibility he would run into some of them as he searched last night's camp site.

He thought of the two men who would be leaving at midnight. Stillwell was about Jamey Burns's age, but he had the experience and Spartan self-control that it would take to get through the Indian lines. Jedediah had heard someone say that when Stillwell was only twelve he had first hired out as a guide to a wagon train. Curly-haired, slender, and without the slightest trace of a beard, he possessed courage, a quick mind, and cold nerve that belied his boyish appearance.

That was the way Jedediah assayed young Stillwell, but Pierre Trudeau was something else. Much older than Stillwell, he was a trapper who had experience to draw on, but he had seemed a queer one from the first. He had been nicknamed "Avalanche" because he insisted on pronouncing the word "ambulance" as if it were "avalanche."

Trudeau had been the butt of more than one joke from some of the smart-alecks of the command, so perhaps he had been impelled to volunteer for this hazardous mission in an effort to attain stature. Jedediah was startled by the thought that possibly the motives which had compelled Forsyth to lead his command into this situation were not much different from those which had induced Trudeau to volunteer to accompany Stillwell.

"By God, you got no call to sit there on your ass that way," Harney burst out. "Git over here and help me. You'd better git something down your gullet, too, if you don't want to starve to death."

Jedediah took the proffered strip of raw meat from Harney and put it into his mouth. His stomach rebelled, but he kept chewing until he got it down. Taking his knife, he set to work beside Harney, keeping at it until the last bit of light had left the sky.

Chapter 19

WHEN it was dark enough so that he could be moved safely, Louis Farley was carried to the center of the island and placed in a pit with the rest of the wounded. He and his son Hudson had taken a position at the extreme low end of the island, and it had not been possible to reach them during the daylight hours. The elder Farley had received a severe thigh wound. Hudson had been less severely wounded in his shoulder, but in spite of their wounds, both had done more than their share of fighting.

When Harney heard about the Farleys, he said indifferently, "Every man on the island's a hero 'cept Burns. Nuthin' for old Lou to do but lie there and shoot."

Jedediah could not dismiss the Farleys that lightly, particularly Louis, whose wound was both dangerous and painful. The events of the day had measured every man on the island unmercifully. Jamey Burns, with his abject cowardice, was one extreme. Louis Farley, the way Jedediah saw it, was the other. Forsyth, too, for in spite of three wounds, he was still the commanding officer.

Hudson Farley was about the same age as Jamey Burns and Jack Stillwell. The fact that he had acquitted himself well was another tribute to his father, Jedediah thought, just as Jamey's actions were an indictment of his parents. For that reason Jamey was not entirely to blame, and Jedediah felt compassion for him, although he knew he was the only man in the command who did.

Shortly after Louis Farley was moved word came that Fred Beecher had died. Jedediah had expected it all day. Still, the news was a shock to him. As long as a man was breathing, there was always the chance that a miracle might happen, but once he was dead there was no chance at all.

Working by feel in the rain with his knife and tin pan, Jedediah thought about Beecher as he dug a trench from his and Harney's pit to Jamey's. Jedediah felt as if he had lost a personal friend. He was convinced that every other man on the island shared his feeling.

Shortly before midnight he reached the trench that Jamey was digging from the other side. Putting a hand on the boy's shoulder, he found that Jamey was shivering uncontrollably, probably from fear as much as from the chilling rain.

"Stillwell and Trudeau are going for help," Jedediah said. "A relief column should reach us in six days."

"They won't get through," Jamey cried. "We're all going to die right here on this island. I wish I was home."

"I guess we all do," Jedediah said, thinking that it would be cruel to remind Jamey that he had done all he could to make him stay home. "Better get some sleep. We'll have more fighting tomorrow and we won't have Stillwell's and Trudeau's rifles to help us. We'll need yours."

He returned to his pit. Presently Stillwell called, "Jones."

"Here," Jedediah said. "Walk easy or you'll fall into our trench."

"That's why I hollered," Stillwell said.

A moment later Stillwell and Trudeau crawled into the pit, Harney appearing from the other side where he had been digging.

"Takin' some meat?" Harney asked.

"All we figure we can carry," Stillwell said. "God, it's dark as a bull's gut."

"You're lucky it is," Harney said. "You're lucky it's rainin', too. It'll make it tougher for 'em to track you. Another thing—was I you, I'd wear my blanket around me so if one of 'em goes by while you're walkin', he'll think it's just another Injun."

"We thought of that," Stillwell said, "though as dark as it is, I doubt if it will make any difference."

Stillwell and Trudeau sat down and, pulling off their boots, tied the laces together and hung them around their necks. Pliley, who was the sentry on the south side of the island, joined them and they shook hands. Pliley said, "Good luck." Jedediah added, "God go with you," and was surprised at himself for saying it. Harney said, "You can make it if you don't get in a hurry and try movin' in daylight. They'll get you sure if you do."

"Slow and easy does it," Stillwell said, laughing softly. "Kind o' funny when you think about it. We ride to hellan-gone trying to find Indians, and then when we do find them, Avalanche and me have to walk back."

Stillwell and Trudeau eased off the island. Walking backwards as Harney had suggested, they disappeared into the darkness. Pliley said in a low tone, "There go two good men."

"You'll be next," Harney said.

"Maybe so," Pliley agreed. "Chances are it'll take more'n two men to get to Fort Wallace. I don't think a man's got much show out there, but I'll tackle it tomorrow night if the Colonel wants me to. I'd just as soon die walking as to do it sitting here."

They waited, ears straining for any sound that might indicate Stillwell and Trudeau had run into trouble, but they heard nothing except the occasional rumble of talk from some of the men on the island and the constant death chant of the squaws from the bluffs.

It seemed to Jedediah that these next few hours would be the darkest, with the rain still coming down and the clouds showing no tendency to break away, so the two men would probably make their best time during those hours. On the other hand, crossing the mile of flat land before they reached the ridge was the most dangerous mile they would travel, because that was where they would be most likely to run into Indians. If they once reached the ridge and found a hiding place for the day, they had a chance of getting through.

Presently Jedediah said, "Pliley, I have the Colonel's permission to leave the island to hunt for anything we can use. A shovel or a kettle—maybe even the medical supplies."

"The medical supplies are gone," Pliley said, "but you might find a shovel or kettle. We could use both."

"You damned fool," Harney said. "Have you got to be a hero too? Ain't Stillwell and Trudeau enough heroes for us tonight?"

"The way I feel all squeezed up inside," Jedediah said, "I'm a long ways from being a hero."

"Take your knife and revolver with you," Pliley said. "If you get into trouble, you'll have to fight out of it by yourself. The Colonel didn't give anyone else permission to leave the island."

"I don't expect any help," Jedediah said. "All I'm asking is that you don't shoot me when I come back."

"I won't," Pliley said, "but somebody else might. That's the chance you're taking."

For a moment Jedediah hesitated, feeling like a man trying to work up enough nerve to dive into a deep, ice-cold pool of water. The longer he waited, the harder it would be to start, so he stepped off the bank into the sand and angled to his right, the opposite direction to that which Stillwell and Trudeau had taken. When he reached the south bank, he dropped belly-flat into the grass and waited, listening.

Hearing nothing that alarmed him, he continued on his hands and knees, often dropping flat again to listen. A new danger occurred to him. Suppose he got his sense of direction twisted and failed to find the island when he returned? He might have to wait until daylight. If he found himself some distance from the island, he would have small chance of reaching it. In the morning the Indians would be swarming all over the valley again, and they'd like nothing better than to pick up a straggler. He went on, trying not to think of the things that might happen to him. Compared to what Stillwell and Trudeau were doing, this was small risk indeed.

He thought he had covered approximately the distance to the camp site of the previous night when he reached forward and felt a pile of ashes instead of the grass through which he had been moving. It might be the remains of his and Redig's fire; it might be any of a dozen others. He had no way of knowing, but at least he was sure now that he was where he wanted to be.

Turning right, he crawled parallel to the south bank of the stream, knowing that this was the way the camp had lay, but he had no way of determining whether the ashes he'd found had been from the end fire or one in the middle.

Within the next few minutes he found the remains of two more fires. Not finding any more, he reversed himself and crawled back, this time keeping a few feet closer to the creek, his hands searching the grass on both sides of him.

This was like the proverbial search for a needle in a haystack. If he did find anything that was useful it would be sheer accident, for he had no way of knowing where anything was dropped in the helter-skelter rush for the island that morning.

A moment later his outflung hand touched the smooth, wet end of a shovel handle. He gripped it exultantly and pulled it to him, his breath coming in gusty pants, his heart pounding.

The feeling of exultation lasted only a few seconds. Someone was coming directly toward him. He couldn't make out the moving figure, but he caught the soft whisper of a foot falling in the wet grass, then another and another.

For an instant he was terrified by the thought that he had to kill whoever this was. He couldn't take the risk of not killing him, yet it might be one of the scouts. He couldn't call out and ask. He couldn't risk using his revolver. There might be a dozen Indians in the area. If he made any sound that was heard for more than a few feet away, he'd draw the whole pack down on him.

A moment later he dismissed the possibility that this was one of the scouts. Forsyth would have informed him if he had given any of the others permission to leave the island. Besides, the steps were not those of a white man's boots. He drew his knife from its sheath and gripped it firmly in his right hand. Sweat broke through his skin to mingle with the cold rain that by now had soaked his clothes.

The steps stopped. He could barely make out the shadowy figure of the Indian, so vague in the darkness that he could not tell whether the warrior was big or small, fat or scrawny.

Apparently the brave had stopped to listen. Jedediah realized gratefully that if he had been moving at this moment, the Indian would have heard him instead of it being the other way. As it was, even lying tense and motionless on the grass, he was afraid the warrior would hear his breathing.

The Indian came on, still moving slowly. By staying flat on the ground, Jedediah was reasonably certain he wouldn't be seen, as dark as it was. The greatest danger was that the Indian might step on him. If he did, he'd have to grab the moccasined foot and bring the warrior down, but the danger was that even if he succeeded in killing him, the fight would make enough noise to bring others.

Another step, then another. Jedediah now lay on his side, his left hand raised a few inches from his body to grab an ankle or a foot. Then, for some reason, the Indian swung sharply toward the creek and took a step in that direction, moving away from Jedediah, his back to him. Some vagrant thought had turned him, or perhaps a sound which had escaped Jedediah.

For a moment Jedediah didn't move, so certain had he been that the Indian was going to pass within inches of him. Then he realized that this was sheer luck, but that he had no time to waste.

He came up off the ground in a rush and hurled himself at the warrior, his left arm swinging out and coming in at what he intended to be chest level. The brave was shorter than he had expected, so his forearm slammed back against the brave's throat, choking off a surprised grunt. In that same instant he drove his knife into the Indian's back.

Jedediah was surprised at how easily the blade went in. The brave went limp in his grasp. With an effort, he yanked the knife free and let the Indian drop. He fell on him, burying the blade in the soft part of the belly. A sibilant rush of air burst out of the brave's lungs. It sounded frighteningly loud to Jedediah. He lifted the knife and slid it into its sheath; he whirled off the body and hunted furiously in the grass for the shovel.

He took a moment to find it, and all the time that he was hunting he was terrified by the thought that fifty Indians might be running across the grass toward him. His right hand fell on the handle. He picked the shovel up and ran toward the island.

He realized immediately this was foolish. If other Indians were close by, the sound of his running would bring them to him. He dropped flat and crawled on hands and knees until he reached the bank of the creek, then he rose and raced across the sand, calling, "Pliley."

He was on the island when he heard Andy Crowell's voice, "Who is it?"

Crowell might shoot, Jedediah thought, and dived headlong into the grass and weeds at the edge of the bank, then he heard Pliley running toward him, saying, "It's Jones. Don't shoot."

Sleeping men roused and began asking questions. Pliley quieted them by assuring them it was all right, that it was Jones returning to the island from the south bank.

Crowell said shakily, "I almost let him have it. What were you doing out there, Slim?"

"Hunting for a shovel," Jedediah said. "I found one, too."

"Good," Pliley said. "You know, I thought Crowell was going to plug you before you or I could get him stopped."

"So did I," Jedediah said.

"Well, get back to your pit," Pliley said. "Might as well sleep when you can."

From the location of Crowell's rifle pit, Jedediah knew he had reached the island a few feet downstream from where he had left it. When he got back to his trench, Harney said sleepily, "A hell of a lot of noise. So you got a shovel?"

"Yes."

"Kill any Indians?"

"One."

"Well now, by God, you're a fighting man. Or you're lucky. Hard to tell which."

"Just lucky," Jedediah said.

He put his back against the side of the pit, shivering. He was wet and cold, but he was trembling because he was afraid, now that it was over. Or perhaps his shakes were the natural reaction from stabbing a man to death. He would never forget how it felt to drive that knife into the Indian's back, then pull it free and sink it into the belly of a man who was probably already dead.

He lay there, eyes closed, thinking he could not sleep, but he dropped off in a few minutes. He did not waken until the first sunlight was in his eyes. The clouds had broken away. This would be another hot day.

So the long vigil began, the waiting for rescue or death.

Chapter 20

JEDEDIAH could not stand upright and stretch as he wanted to. Even at this early hour the Indian sharpshooters were in the grass and firing again, so he remained flat in the sand. Putting his arms above his head, he stretched and yawned, then sat up, his back against the side of the pit.

He was stiff and sore, his damp clothes clinging to him. Sand was everywhere, in his ears and between his teeth and down his back. He wondered if he would ever be free of it again.

He did not disturb Harney, who was snoring on the other side of the pit, oblivious to the crackling of rifle fire from across the creek. Jedediah was so hungry that even a breakfast of raw horse meat seemed palatable.

Working his way past Reddy's body to the carcass of Harney's horse, he sliced a strip of meat from a hind quarter and returned to the pit. Using his knife that was still stained with the blood of the Indian he had killed the night before, he cut mouthfuls of meat from the strip. He chewed each bite the best he could and forced it down, although more than once he gagged and everything he had eaten threatened to come up.

He had a drink of muddy water from his canteen, then settled back as the sun rose above the eastern rim of the earth and warmed him and dried his clothes. Presently

Harney shifted and woke, sand trickling down his shirt. He swore and scratched, then yawned.

"We're still alive," Harney said. "A man in our fix can't ask for nuthin' more." He yawned again. "Well, guess I'll go cut me a slice o' breakfast."

Harney was right, Jedediah thought. This morning none of them could ask anything more. At least six days would pass before they could expect to see a relief column. Perhaps not even then. Stillwell and Trudeau might not be alive right now. Or, if they were, they could not have gone far last night, so they would be hiding out there somewhere in a ravine or a patch of brush or a cave. Anything they could find. But they could not possibly have gone far enough to be out of danger from the roving bands of mounted Indians that were coming and going for no apparent reason.

Would Stillwell and Trudeau be alive by night? If they were, would they be alive by another sunup? Jedediah wondered if two men had ever carried as much of a burden as Stillwell and Trudeau did, out there on the prairie unable to sneeze or cough or take a good, deep breath, the hope for life of every man on the island dependent on their survival.

Later in the morning Forsyth ordered Jedediah and several other men to dig shallow graves for Beecher, Wilson, and Culver. In a short time the hot sun began sucking up the moisture that had fallen during the night. Steam hovered over the valley, giving it the weird appearance of being on fire.

When they finished the burial, Jedediah gave the shovel to Pliley, who wanted to dig the well deeper. He lingered beside the graves, thinking it strange that there had been no funeral ceremony of any sort, not as much as a prayer. But who was to pray? Apparently even Andy Crowell had forgotten the words.

Jedediah remembered what he had said to Stillwell and Trudeau last night. "God go with you." Odd and unfamiliar words coming from his lips. He had never spoken them before. He wasn't sure why he had said them. He had never joined a church; he held no formal belief, unless it was the negative one of not accepting the God Andy Crowell had worshiped so fervently back in the Laura's Tit church, a jealous and vengeful God who had picked Crowell as His spokesman in the community, a God who said that unless a man followed certain forms, such as deep-water baptism, he must spend eternity in hell.

No, that kind of God was an unbelievable monster, inferior even to the Indian notion of a Great Spirit. He must, Jedediah decided, possess some instinctive knowledge of a bigger and finer God than Andy Crowell's, a God who would protect Stillwell and Trudeau through the dangerous hours that lay ahead for them. Or was such knowledge instinctive?

The question nagged at him until he started thinking of his father's teachings about God. It had been a long time ago when he had been very young and his father had loved him and taken care of him, long before his father had sold himself to a hip-switching bitch who stood in front of her cabin and smiled at him when he came home from work.

Jedediah could not remember very much of what his father had taught him about God except that He was a loving and merciful Father who wanted the best for his children, just as Nehemiah Jones had once wanted the best for Jedediah. He wondered wryly what his father believed now. Or was it possible that he did not believe in anything?

Suddenly it struck him, and the knowledge surprised him, that he could think of his father without hatred. He was capable even of being grateful for the years they'd had together, for the fact that his father had taken care of him until he could look out for himself.

This was the first time in nine years that the memory of his father had not brought with it the poison of hatred. Still, the memory did not bring pleasure to his mind, so he consciously turned his thoughts to Cally. He wanted to stand upright and cry out that he had to live, he had to go back and see Cally and tell her he had been wrong, that he loved her more than he could tell her.

Someone yelled, "Indians!" The word was a giant eraser that instantly cleaned the blackboard of his mind. He crawled back to his rifle pit. Harney had been wrong. The scouts would have to fight again today. But a few minutes later Jedediah saw that Harney was right. The first volley of the Spencers scattered the Indians before the attack gained momentum.

Harney scratched a bearded cheek and grinned at Jedediah. He said smugly, "Still goin' just like I told you, Jed. Take Roman Nose out of it and they ain't got much left. I figure this bunch was just tryin' to fetch some o' their dead back to camp and didn't intend to make no big fight. We won't have much trouble if we keep our heads down."

Jedediah wasn't sure whether Harney meant it or not.

Maybe he was trying to keep his courage up. Jedediah discarded the thought immediately. Harney had no need to do anything to keep his courage up. Life had made a fatalist of him. He would meet whatever came when it came, and above everything else he would try to save his own life. He admitted it often enough. So, if he was consciously trying to do anything, it was to keep Jedediah's courage up.

Later in the day dinner was another strip of raw horse meat, another drink of muddy water. Then, sitting in the rifle pit with his back against its wall of sand, he heard Jamey cry out above the distant beating of Indian drums, "Ma! Ma! Where are you, Ma?"

Harney shook his head in disgust. "Why don't I go put him out of his misery? You shoot a horse if he breaks his leg. Might as well be the same with the kid. He's done worse than break his leg."

"No," Jedediah said.

He crawled through the connecting trench to Jamey's rifle pit. The boy was asleep, curled up in the bottom of the pit, his Spencer beside him. Reaching out, Jedediah took Jamey's arm and stirred him awake.

"Your Ma's not here, Jamey," he said. "You wanted to be a man. Why don't you prove that you are one?"

Jamey's eyes opened. He pulled free from Jedediah's grasp and cowered against the wall of his rifle pit. "I can't, Mr. Jones," he moaned. "I know what they think of me. They've got a right to. So have you, but I can't do what I'm supposed to. I just can't."

"You know what Harney says about you?" Jedediah asked. "He says you'll hate yourself the rest of your life unless you start acting like a man. I think he's right."

"It doesn't make any difference," Jamey said. "We're all going to die here anyway."

Jedediah left him then. Harney had been right about a good many things. Maybe he was right about this. Jamey might be better off dead.

Late in the afternoon Jedediah and Crowell and some of the others gathered brush and arrows that had fallen on the island and built a fire. They boiled several pieces of horse meat in a pickle jar that Forsyth found in his saddlebag, and gave the meat to the wounded. Dr. Mooers was still alive, but Jedediah held no hope for him. The other wounded, he thought, might make it.

He welcomed this chance to do something to break the

monotony of waiting. Six days of this would make them all go crazy, he thought. Redig had moved to the other side of the island and dug another rifle pit. He fired occasionally at a mounted Indian between the island and the bluffs, but none came within range, so the ammunition was wasted. Still the Indian snipers stayed in the grass using their rifles and bows and arrows; still the beating of the drums and the death chants went on.

Supper offered no variety. A piece of raw horse meat, a drink of water from Jedediah's canteen. At dusk he wrote in his diary: *The end of the second day. No one was wounded today. No one else has died. We are in a state of siege. The victor will be the side with the greatest staying power, but which side will that be?*

Pliley and Whitney agreed to make a try at working through the Indian lines. At ten o'clock they started for Fort Wallace. Jedediah was on guard duty when they returned at 3 A.M., calling to him so he wouldn't fire. After they crossed the stream to the island, Pliley told Jedediah, "Nobody could get through their lines tonight. We couldn't do anything but come back."

"They either caught Stillwell and Trudeau," Whitney added, "or they picked up their tracks and know they got through. Anyhow, they were watching for us tonight."

After Pliley and Whitney went on to report to Forsyth, Jedediah stood with his Spencer in his hand, staring into the darkness toward the ridge line to the south. Were Stillwell and Trudeau still out there, alive and moving? Or had they been caught and tortured to death? The answer was hidden by the night blackness. For Jedediah and the others there was nothing to do but wait and hope.

While he stood there, he heard Andy Crowell's voice: "Oh God, I beseech Thee to save Thy servant from these savages. Lord, strike them down as the Philistines were once struck down. Give me the strength of Samson . . ."

Crowell was still praying as Jedediah walked away, Crowell's words bringing a bitter taste to his mouth. He spat over the bank into the sand and rubbed a palm across his mouth as he wondered if Crowell honestly thought God would strike down the savages just to save him.

When he was relieved of guard duty, Jedediah returned to his pit and fell asleep at once. Dawn came slowly, for the sky was covered by an overcast, the pale light trickling out across the plains as if it were strained thin by the bank of clouds.

When he woke, his first thought was that this would be another long day of tedious waiting, and then the question: What had happened to Trudeau and Stillwell?

Chapter 21

JEDEDIAH was thankful that the third day stayed cool, for he knew how the wounded, many of them feverish, had suffered under the hot sun of the previous day. The Indians made no move to attack, although a small party did ride toward the island, the warrior in the lead holding a white flag.

"Don't let 'em get any closer," Grover shouted. "You can't trust the bastards."

"Sign to them to keep back," Forsyth said. "This is no peace commission. Shoot the first red devil that comes within range."

Grover rose, motioned them back, and dropped flat again. The Indians withdrew. Harney said angrily, "Now that's a damn shame. There's three bodies yonder the Injuns haven't been able to get. That's all this bunch wanted. They're afraid we'll scalp 'em, and they sure don't want that to happen. Wouldn't hurt us to tell 'em come on up and get the carcasses."

A queer thing, Jedediah thought. The scouts were pinned down by the Indians, perhaps to die of starvation, and yet Bill Harney did not hate them. Probably every other man on the island agreed with Forsyth and Grover, but Harney would have let them recover their dead.

Perhaps Harney would die at the hands of the Indians. Still, he had compassion for them. A strange man, this Braggin' Bill Harney, a man completely beyond Jedediah's understanding. If Harney was more savage than civilized, as he had judged him to be, it would be a good thing, Jedediah decided, if all civilized men were a little bit more savage.

Jedediah was talking to Forsyth at noon when it was apparent that the women and children were leaving the bluffs to the north.

"They're giving up the fight," Forsyth said jubilantly.

"We'll get two men through tonight. Jones, go get Pliley and Whitney."

Within a few minutes Jedediah was back in Forsyth's pit with Whitney and Pliley. Forsyth had taken his memorandum book and a pencil from his saddlebag and had written a message to Colonel Bankhead at Fort Wallace.

"I think you men can make it tonight," he said. "I have a dispatch message for you to deliver to Colonel Bankhead. We have no way of knowing what has happened to Stillwell and Trudeau. All we know is that if they didn't get through, we'll die here if we don't send someone else."

"I'll try," Pliley said. "I don't think the Indians are giving up, but some of them are bound to drift away, so we'll have fewer of them watching the island. That'll give us a better chance." He nodded at Whitney. "He's bunged up with rheumatism. I'd better find another man to go with me."

"I'm sorry," Whitney said apologetically, "but getting wet the other night played hell with my rheumatism. I guess I should have thought about it before I signed up."

"You're a little late," Forsyth said. "All right, Pliley, see if you can find another man."

"I think Jack Donovan will tackle it," Pliley said.

Forsyth lay back in his pit. "He's a good man," he said, and closed his eyes. The three men drifted away, Jedediah wondering how any man with wounds as serious as Forsyth's could live until relief came.

At dusk he wrote in his diary: *We have survived the third day. Two more men will leave at midnight. The horses are beginning to smell. When I look at Reddy's stiff-legged, bloated body, I wonder why I was so sentimental about it.*

He was asleep when Pliley and Donovan slipped away from the island. When he woke the next morning, he saw that Harney was just returning from guard duty. He said, "Didn't hear no shootin' or yellin' out yonder last night. I figger Pliley and Donovan made it."

The fourth day had started. Jedediah stared up at the steadily brightening sky and thought of Stillwell and Trudeau, who perhaps had left too soon, when the Indians had been at their greatest strength. Probably the two men were dead long before this. But did it make any difference when they died? Even if they had been tortured by the Indians, was their fate worse than a death by starvation?

He rubbed his face with his hands and sat up. Pliley and Donovan had started too late, he thought now. They could not bring help in time, even if they succeeded in getting to Fort Wallace. Forsyth had said the scouts could hold out for six days. Two more! There was no way under the sun in which two men on foot could reach the fort and bring help back in that time.

"Better eat your breakfast," Harney said. "You ain't gonna make it if you don't eat."

"What difference does it make?" Jedediah asked. "Help can't get here in time."

"Sure it can," Harney said. "We've got water—that's the main thing. Don't start figgerin' that Forsyth knows everything. We can hang on more'n the six days he gave us. You can count on it."

Harney believed it. Again hope burned brightly in Jedediah's mind. Harney was the most practical man on the island. If he believed they could hold out for more than six days, they could. Jedediah did not doubt it, a certainty which gave him the strength to force down another strip of tainted meat.

A short time later he heard that Dr. Mooers had finally died. He was the fourth man. Without medical supplies, some of the other wounded would die. Their wounds would become infected, gangrene would set it, and nothing could save them.

Jedediah and Crowell dug the surgeon's grave. When they had finished, Forsyth called them to him. He had taken his razor from his saddlebag and now held it up to Jedediah.

"Your hands are steady, Jones," Forsyth said. "I can't stand that bullet in my thigh. Take it out."

Forsyth had sliced his pants and drawers over the wound so that it was exposed. Jedediah looked at the bullet hole and shook his head. He had some idea of the agony the ball was causing Forsyth, but it lay too close to the femoral artery for anyone except a surgeon to remove it. A slight slip of the razor blade and the artery would be cut, and nothing could save Forsyth from bleeding to death.

"I don't know much about surgery," Jedediah said, "but I know enough to be afraid to try it. It's too close to the artery."

Forsyth swore, and bit his lower lip against the pain. He held the razor out to Crowell. "You do it. I tell you I can't stand it."

Crowell shook his head. "I'm a farmer, Colonel. I've done lots of butchering and I know what it means to cut an artery. I'm afraid to try it."

Forsyth lay back, his eyes closed, fighting his pain and his temper. McCall and Grover and several others had gathered beside the pit, but when Forsyth sat up, he could not persuade any of them to remove the bullet.

"None of us want to be responsible for your cashing in, Colonel," McCall said. "That's what will happen if we take that bullet out."

"Then I'll take it out myself," Forsyth said sharply. "Jones, will you and Crowell press the flesh back? Surely you can do that much?"

Jedediah hesitated, then nodded at Crowell, who nodded back. "All right, I guess we can do that."

Jedediah bent over Forsyth from one side, Crowell on the other, hands pressing against the flesh of his thigh. The pressure must have intensified the agony that Forsyth was suffering, but he gave no indication of it. He bent forward, and began slicing lengthwise over the bullet hole. He worked slowly and carefully, his face ghastly.

A moment later the ball, under the pressure of Jedediah's and Crowell's fingers, popped out of the thigh with a small spurt of blood. Forsyth lay back, gray of face and close to fainting, while Jedediah laid a wet dressing on the wound. The cloth partially stopped the bleeding. It would soon clot, Jedediah thought. There was no danger of serious bleeding now. If the razor had slashed the artery, the blood would be pumping from the cut in great spurts.

Jedediah and Crowell moved back from Forsyth, Jedediah glancing at McCall, who was staring at Forsyth's ashen face. "By God, Colonel," McCall said in a low voice, "you're a man."

"Anything was better than the pain it was giving me," Forsyth said. "It feels better now."

The afternoon dragged out, each hour seeming to Jedediah to plod by. None of the scouts fired a shot except Redig, who swore that he saw some mounted Cheyennes who had come within rifle range.

"He's gone clean crazy," Harney said. "Forsyth ought to take his ammunition away from him. We may need every shell we've got."

Crazy or not, Forsyth said nothing to Redig. Likely Forsyth thought that an occasional shot from the island was a good thing, Jedediah told himself. At least it was a warning to the Indians that some of the scouts were still alive.

Now the smell from the dead horses was so bad that Jedediah found it hard to breathe. An empty stomach was bad enough, but the constant nauseating stench made it worse.

That night he wrote in his diary: *The end of the fourth day. Only God knows how many more we can stand.*

He closed his eyes and tried to bring Cally's face into focus, but he could not. He wasn't losing his senses, he told himself. Not like Jamey or Redig, or even Andy Crowell, who wanted the Lord to save him but apparently didn't care about anyone else. It was just that he was hungry and tired and terribly sick of the damned stench from which there was no escape.

Chapter 22

HE WOKE ON THE MORNING of the fifth day with the thought that if Forsyth was right, tomorrow would be the end unless a relief column arrived. But if Harney was right, the sixth day would not be the last. He had to be right on this; Jedediah had to believe that he was.

Still, Jedediah found his faith weak. Tomorrow might be the last day of his life. In spite of himself, his gaze wandered time after time to the ridge to the south or to the entrance to the valley from the east. If help ever came, it would be from one of these directions.

Later in the day it became evident that the Indians were withdrawing. The siege was over, but to Jedediah's way of thinking, it was small cause for rejoicing, for actually it made little difference. They were still pinned here on the island; they would starve whether the Indians were around or not. The meat that had been preserved was nearly gone. There was no salt at all, and the need for it was a crying demand in the body of every man on the island.

It was a relief to Jedediah not to have to remain in his rifle pit, to stand upright without being afraid an Indian sniper would blow his head off. Men gathered in knots to talk, the easing of tension almost a tangible feeling in the air. Gradually the men who weren't wounded and the ones who, like Harney, had suffered minor injuries gathered at the lower end of the island far enough from Forsyth's pit so he could not hear them.

Jedediah and Harney were the last to join the crowd. A glance at McCall's stormy face was enough to tell Jedediah that this was trouble. He guessed what it was before he heard a word of the argument. He had been certain that some of the men would want to desert the wounded if the Indians pulled out.

"We don't know that Stillwell and Trudeau made it," one of the scouts was saying. "All we know is that they had damned little chance of getting through. As for Donovan and Pliley, why, hell, they just left too late."

Several of the men nodded. One said, "It looks like a simple proposition to me. We stay here and starve to death, or we start walking. If we walk, some of us will make it. If we stay, we all die. Now is there any sense in that?"

"We can't just go off and leave Pa and Colonel Forsyth and the rest of them that can't walk," Hudson Farley said angrily. "What kind of men are you?"

"I've already told them," McCall said. "They're not men. They have no right to call themselves men."

"It doesn't make any difference what we call ourselves," Jamey Burns said. "If we've got a chance to live by walking, we ought to start."

Jedediah whirled on him, as furious as he had been that first morning when the Indians had shot his sorrel. He slapped Jamey on the side of the face, spinning him half around. "What have you done to earn a chance to live? What good are you to anybody if you do?"

Jamey stared at him in amazement, a hand raised to the side of his face. Jedediah gave him his back. He said, "We've fought together and we'll live or die together. I'll personally shoot the first son-of-a-bitch who walks off this island and starts for Fort Wallace."

McCall turned to him, a tight grin on his stubble-covered face. "That's the kind of talk I like to hear. I've already told them the same thing."

"The bastards may come back," Matthew Redig said. "We might get a chance to kill some more of them if they do. I say we stay."

Harney reared back, his thumbs rammed inside his waistband. He said, "Boys, you all know me. I ain't got no fine notions like Jed has 'bout dyin' together. I just want to live. I ain't fussy 'bout the rest o' you. It's me I'm interested in. If Jed and McCall miss you when they shoot at you, I won't.

"We're stayin' and I'll tell you why, 'cause you ain't got

sense enough to know. If we string out across the prairie on foot we'll scatter out. Some'll walk faster'n others. Sooner or later the Injuns'll spot us and they'll lift the hair of every one of us. Redig's right 'bout 'em comin' back. They might. If they do, the only chance we've got to beat 'em off is for everyone of us to be here shootin'."

Silence then. Some of them dug their toes into the sand. Some scratched themselves. Some swore under their breath. But one thing was certain, Jedediah thought as his gaze moved from one to the other. Harney's word carried more weight than anyone else's. He had never made any pretense of being anything but a selfish man who wanted to survive. If staying on the island meant survival for him, then it must mean survival to everyone else.

"McCall," Forsyth shouted. "I want to talk to the men. Bring them here—all of them."

McCall jerked his head in the direction of Forsyth's rifle pit. "Get over there, all of you, and I hope he takes your hide off."

But Forsyth didn't. He raised himself on an elbow to stare at the men who stood grouped before him. Some of them wore bloody bandages; all were dirty, sweat-crusted, stubble-faced, and hungry.

"We're not a pretty lot," Forsyth said, "but we're fighters. We've proved that. It is my understanding that there has been some talk about trying to reach Fort Wallace and leave the wounded here. I won't try to keep you here indefinitely, but it is your duty as soldiers, your duty to humanity, to stay at least long enough to give the men who left here for the fort a chance to reach it and send help to us. After that time has passed, I have no more claim on you. You'll be welcome to do whatever you think you should to save your lives."

"We're staying," Jedediah said.

"That's right, Colonel," McCall agreed. "We've been through a hell of a lot together. We won't break up now."

"Good." Forsyth lay back in his pit, tired, his face bright with fever. "I couldn't ask for more from any command."

They broke up then, Jedediah not sure whether the grumblers were satisfied or not, but he heard no more talk of leaving the island. That night he wrote briefly in his diary: *We have survived the fifth day. It is not only our empty stomachs that bother us now. The stink of rotting horse flesh is all around us. I have never smelled anything so bad, but there is nothing we can do about it.*

He considered writing about the threatened desertion, then decided not to. Nothing could be gained. He slipped the diary and pencil back into his pocket, thinking that if they lived, they would all be heroes on the pages of history. If they died, they would still be heroes and no one need ever know the truth. Let the legend about them grow. The thought amused him that the historians seldom wrote about the cowards, perhaps because their readers only wanted to read about the heroes.

The sixth day was worse than any of the others because this was the day that ended the time Forsyth had said they could last. But they still lived. The stench was worse. The flies were worse. The coyotes were worse. Lured by the smell of festering horse flesh, they had surrounded the island during the night and howled hour after hour. The guards shot at them, but in the darkness only a miracle would have scored a hit, and there seemed to be no miracles in the making.

As Jedediah thought about it, he decided that a miracle was taking place. No one had died. Kettles were found and brought to the island from the camp site south of the creek. Fires were built and chunks of horse meat boiled and the soup fed to those who were suffering the most. Maggots had infected some of the wounds. The first evidence of gangrene was appearing. Still the wounded lived.

When Jedediah wasn't helping with the wounded, he was watching the ridge line to the south, asking himself how much longer it would take for the relief party to get here. By nightfall no help had come.

That evening he wrote in his diary: *We have lived through six days of this. I wonder if I can ever get this sickening stench out of my nostrils. I have forgotten what a breath of clean air is like. Our preserved meat is gone. We have nothing to eat except rotting horse flesh which has green streaks running through it. When we cut into it, the smell is worse. I constantly wonder that any of us are alive.*

He replaced the diary and pencil in his pocket. Harney was on guard duty. Jedediah was satisfied to be alone. He always felt better when he could think of Cally; when he could picture her face in his mind, but still it wouldn't come clear and he wasn't sure why.

He closed his eyes and dropped off to sleep in spite of the stench. He woke suddenly, feeling that Cally was with him. He had clearly heard her voice just as he had that last evening he had been with her when she had quoted John Donne: "No man is an island, entire of itself."

He knew now how right she was; but more important, he realized how smug he had been with his book learning, how smug and how ignorant. But what was his destiny? Why was he alive and Fred Beecher dead? Had the Lord decided he must learn a lesson in this hard way?

Impulsively he cried out, "I've learned it, God. How much longer must I keep on learning it?"

"What did you say, Mr. Jones?" Jamey asked from his rifle pit.

"Nothing, Jamey," he answered. "I guess I was dreaming."

But he hadn't been. Now he could not sleep. He lay there staring at the star-lighted sky, but no answers came to him.

Chapter 23

ANOTHER day, each hour of it dragging out into what seemed an eternity to Jedediah. The sand, the sun beating down upon both the wounded and the well, a diet of horse flesh that stunk so badly he could not put it into his mouth without gagging, the constant scrutiny of the ridge to the south, watching for the help that never came. This was the way it had been, the way it would be again today.

To Jedediah the smell was the worst of all, the effluvium from the dead horses that hung over the island like a noxious cloud. The stink seemed to get worse by the hour, although he wondered how anything as bad as this stench could get worse. It was everywhere: in his nostrils, on his hands, on his clothes. There was no escape from it.

He did what he could for the wounded, along with Crowell and the others, but there was little any of them could do to relieve the suffering. Change the water dressings, wash the wounds that were shallow enough to wash, give a drink of water from a canteen, and try to be cheerful. The latter was the hardest. How could any man be cheerful in the face of a slow and what seemed inevitable death, a death that appeared to be more certain with each passing hour?

Jedediah noticed that Andy Crowell talked very little.

For days he had said nothing to the men about saving their souls, and if he had any hope of eternal salvation for himself, he said nothing about it to anyone. Jamey huddled in his rifle pit, pathetic and lost, feeling the contempt of every man on the island. Matthew Redig roamed restlessly, the only one who watched for Indians and not for the relief column. To Jedediah the most amazing man on the island was Forsyth. In spite of his wounds and consuming fever, he still held by sheer strength of will to his right to command.

Hope had been a tenuous thread at best, and now Jedediah sensed that it had steadily decreased in everyone except Braggin' Bill Harney. This seventh day was one more day than Forsyth had said they could hold out, and still no one else had died. If relief came now, perhaps no one else would, although Louis Farley's thigh wound was in terrible shape.

Jedediah felt like a hypocrite when he assured the wounded that help would come tomorrow. That was the way it had been for days, always tomorrow because help had not come today. But there was no hypocrisy in Harney, who went around seemingly as strong as ever. He talked cheerfully about what he was going to do after they were rescued. He never gave the slightest encouragement to those who said they were destined to die here.

"Hell, no, we ain't gonna die on this damn island," Harney said over and over. "We can hold on a long time yet. Bankhead's goin' to get here sooner or later."

When Jedediah heard him talk that way, he was ashamed of his own lack of faith. He thought about death; he could not escape thinking of it, for death surrounded him even in the sickening stench from the horses. Four men had died. Farley probably would die in a few days. The wounded would go. Then the ones who were not injured, giving up one by one under the steadily increasing weakness of hunger.

Jedediah was surprised to realize that he did not fear death. Forsyth didn't, either, and perhaps it was his lack of fear which gave him courage. Harney was the same; he had faced death too often to be afraid of it now. But others did, Jamey Burns particularly. Andy Crowell did not talk about it, but Jedediah sensed that he was almost as frantic in his fear of death as Jamey was.

So the seventh day dragged out its interminable length, with only a few bright spots to vary the monotony of the waiting. One of the men made a lucky shot and killed a coyote. The animal was skinned, then boiled and boiled again, with even the marrow sucked from the bones.

Several men, including Jedediah, wandered off the island in search of something, of anything, to eat. Several returned with prickly pear, some of which was boiled down to a kind of syrup. Jedediah found a few wild plums. He stewed them and gave them to the wounded, hardly more than a mouthful apiece.

At dusk he settled back in his rifle pit, his stomach hurting from hunger or from the fearful smelling horse flesh he had forced into it. He wrote in his diary: *The seventh day has passed and we have not been rescued. How much longer will it be?* He had not realized he was so weak until he looked at his shaky handwriting.

That night his stomach kept him awake for hours. Or was it the smell? No man could separate the stink from anything else. The stench was everywhere, a sickening cloud that poisoned the air. Death and hunger and the smell all flowed together, making a horrible nightmare from which there was no awakening.

The sun came up on the eighth day, an event which was surprising to Jedediah because he was alive to see it. In a desperate search of his haversack he found a bacon rind. He chewed on it, finding in the salt it contained the most delightful taste he had ever experienced. With the others, he poured gunpowder on the rotten horse meat to make it less nauseating, but it was of little help, and did not relieve his craving for salt.

When he thought he had chewed the bacon rind until there was no taste left, he threw it away. Crowell found it, and picking it up, chewed on it as gratefully as Jedediah had. When he threw it away, it fell by sheer accident into Jamey's rifle pit. He instantly put it into his mouth and began chewing, his entire body trembling as he closed his eyes and worked the tiny piece of rind back and forth between his teeth.

Jedediah and most of the others who could walk scattered over the valley searching for food. One man gratefully picked up a few grains of coffee that had been spilled the first night they had camped on the south bank of the stream, and made a weak brew from it. Several men had opportunities to shoot coyotes, but no one else brought one in. Jedediah stumbled upon a prairie dog village, but the little animals refused to make an appearance.

The day dragged out as the others had, the men watching, help still not coming, with only Harney confident that it would. "It's a hell of a long ways to Fort Wallace," he said, "but some of the boys got there. You'll see."

But hope at such a time was a fragile thing, so fragile that Jedediah wrote in his diary: *The eighth day has gone and no help has come. Has God deserted us?*

He thought about that question after he had slipped his diary into his pocket. No, God never deserted anyone. For some strange reason he was more confident of that now than he had ever been in his life, but it seemed beside the point. Man makes his choice, Jedediah told himself, and certain results inevitably follow that choice. God, by his very nature, was outside the picture once the choice was made.

Then, because his mind was running clear and sharp at this particular moment, he remembered another question he had asked himself a few days before. What was his destiny, and why had an Indian bullet found Fred Beecher while he, Jedediah Jones, still lived?

He had an answer now. Maybe it wasn't the right answer, but it was one that might do. Every man was born for a purpose, born to do a definite thing. Beecher had done his. Jedediah hadn't, so he would live. He had no idea what he had been born to do, but he would know when the time came, and with that thought hope came again to him.

Just before he dropped off into a troubled sleep, he wondered what Cally would think of such a notion, if his destiny was so bound up with hers that he was spared to go back to her and marry her and give her children? It seemed ridiculous, but he knew that if he was spared, that was exactly what he would do.

He rose at dawn of the ninth day. He remembered this was September 25, but he had forgotten which day of the week it was. Even Sunday had gone by unnoticed.

Taking his Spencer, he slipped away from the island and walked to the prairie dog village, hoping to find some of the small animals out of their holes. If he could shoot only one, he would make soup out of it for the wounded. Any kind of meat, even a tiny prairie dog, would make a thin broth and be far better than the sickening soup that had been made yesterday from putrid horse flesh.

He watched until the middle of the morning, but none of the dogs appeared. Disheartened, he returned to camp, walking slowly, for there was little strength left in him. As he approached the island, he saw that Harney and Crowell and most of the others who could stand were on their feet staring at the ridge behind him.

"Something's movin' over yonder," Harney called. "Git to humpin', Jed. Might be Injuns comin' in for the kill."

Jedediah started to run, and fell, his knees buckling under him. He got up and stumbled across the south channel, the bitter knowledge riding him that if the moving objects were Indians, it was the finish. No one on the island, unless it was Bill Harney, had enough strength left to shoot straight. The Indians would ride them down in the first charge.

He reached the bank of the island and turned to stand beside Crowell, his hand shading his eyes. Jamey was out of his rifle pit staring at the ridge. Glancing at him, Jedediah saw that his thin, dirty face was bright with hope for the first time since the morning they had been attacked.

Jedediah rubbed his eyes and looked at the ridge again, surprised that Jamey, of all the men on the island, would sense that this was the relief column, not the enemy. What did Jamey have to live for, Jamey who could never escape the shame of his miserable cowardice? It was even more surprising that he, Jedediah Jones, who had so much to live for, had accepted Harney's suggestion that they were seeing Indians.

Suddenly Jedediah's heart gave a great bound and he cried out, "It's the relief column! I can see an ambulance."

"By God, he's right!" Harney bellowed. "That's an ambulance, all right, and you never seen no band of Injuns fetchin' an ambulance along. You hear, Colonel? We made it."

"I hear," Forsyth said, his voice thin and very tired.

Harney slapped Jedediah on the back and Jedediah whirled to Andy Crowell and hugged him and danced him off the bank into the sand. He let go, and with the others—ragged, hungry, dirty scarecrows—raised his hat above his head and waved it as he cheered.

He put his hat back on his head and stood motionless, tears flowing down his stubble-covered face, and he was not ashamed. Most of the others were crying, too. This was the unexpected gift of life being brought to them by the relief column that galloped down the ridge and across the flat, for by all the laws of logic every man on the island should be dead.

When the column was close enough, Jedediah recognized Donovan riding in the lead beside Colonel Carpenter, a colored troop of the Tenth Cavalry strung out behind them.

So it was Donovan and Pliley who had made it through the Indian lines, not Stillwell and Trudeau.

Jedediah glanced back at Jamey, who stood on the bank apart from the others, his head bowed, a lonely and pathetic figure.

Donovan and Carpenter reached them and dismounted. Most of the men rushed toward the troopers begging for something to eat, but Jedediah remained where he was to shake hands with Donovan, then with Carpenter, who asked, "Is Colonel Forsyth alive?"

Jedediah nodded. "He's alive, but he was wounded three times."

"Dr. Fitzgerald is with us," Carpenter said. "He'll take care of him."

"What about Pliley?" Jedediah asked.

"At the fort," Donovan answered. "He was too all in to make it back here. We ran into Colonel Carpenter's party that was out on a scout, or we wouldn't have got back this soon."

"God, the stink," Carpenter muttered as they strode toward Forsyth's rifle pit. "We'll get everybody moved as soon as we can."

When they reached Forsyth, he laid down a ragged copy of *Oliver Twist* that he had been reading and held up a claw-like hand to Carpenter. He said, "Welcome to Beecher's Island, Colonel."

That evening, with camp moved far enough from the island to escape the stench, Jedediah wrote in his diary: *The relief column arrived this morning. I cannot find words to describe the ecstasy we felt when we recognized the troopers, nor can I describe how coffee and the usually despised hardtack can be a banquet, or the feeling that comes from knowing I will live when I thought I must die. Louis Farley did. The doctor took off his leg and he could not stand the strain. The doctor said that 24 more hours would have meant he could not have saved Forsyth, but now he believes he can. None of the others are in serious danger. Tonight I thank God just to be alive.*

Part Three

THE LONG ROAD HOME

Chapter 24

JEDEDIAH reached Fort Wallace with the rest of the scouts on September 30. A short time later Sheridan wired an order to give any of the scouts a job in the quartermaster's department for which they were qualified. But this offer did not appeal to Jedediah. He didn't want to stay with the command, which was being reorganized under Lieutenant Papoon, either. So, along with Crowell and Harney and some others, he resigned and waited impatiently for a horse to replace Reddy.

Not that the sorrel could be replaced. To Jedediah Reddy was a casualty of the battle just as Lieutenant Beecher and the other men who had been killed were casualties, but this was a feeling he could not have explained to anyone and he didn't try. There was no need to—it was important only to him. In any case, he needed a horse because he was anxious to return to Laura's Tit.

Jamey Burns was the first to leave, having been discharged for cause. Jedediah was the only one who shook hands with him. Harney was probably right in saying the boy would never amount to a damn from now on. Still, Jedediah was not willing to give up on him, and he could not keep from saying, "You had your chance on the island and you threw it away. Sometimes a man is given another chance. Maybe you will be. If you are, it's up to you what you do with it."

"I know." Jamey stared at the ground, tears running down his cheeks; then he looked up and swallowed and said gratefully, "Thank you for shaking hands with me, Mr. Jones."

He mounted and rode away, Jedediah staring at his back. If anyone ever needed a friend, it was Jamey Burns, but what could friendship do for him? Nothing, Jedediah decided, for a man's salvation came from within. Perhaps Andy Crowell understood that now.

Matthew Redig left soon after Jamey. Jedediah called to him, wanting to shake hands with him, but Redig acted as if he didn't hear. He kept riding, not once looking back. He was like a sleepwalker, and sometimes Jedediah had thought that was exactly what he was.

A strange thing, Jedediah reflected. You join a group of men, most of whom you have never seen before. You go down into the valley of the shadow of death with them and you leave some of them there, and then you break up and scatter, maybe never to see the others again. But each has left some kind of impression upon the rest, and none who survived will ever be quite the same as he had been the morning of September 17 before the first shot was fired.

"You're thinkin' again, Jed," Harney said as he rode up and dismounted. "You think too damned much. I used to watch you on the island when we didn't have nuthin' to do but sit there and smell them stinkin' horses, and by God, you was thinkin' all the time. I say there ain't that much in the world worth thinkin' about."

Jedediah grinned. "I disagree, Bill. There's quite a bit to think about."

"Not that much," Harney growled. "Just ain't worth the trouble. Well, I'm pullin' out. Wanted to shake hands afore I done it. I reckon you'll be ridin' east?"

Jedediah nodded. "Crowell's going with me. I'm waiting for him now."

Harney scratched his nose as if trying to decide what to say. He was still bearded, still dirty, but the slack skin of his face had filled out so he looked less like an animated scarecrow than he had the day the relief column had arrived. If any man had been left unchanged by those nine days, it was Braggin' Bill Harney.

Harney nodded at Stillwell, who was talking to Pliley at the other end of the row of tents. "Funny how a man's stick floats sometimes. When I seen Donovan ridin' in that mornin' with Carpenter, I says to myself that Stillwell and Trudeau had lost their hair, but damned if they didn't make it."

"They got to the fort and gave Bankhead the word," Jedediah said, "and then Bankhead took the long way around just like Grover said to do, but Carpenter came straight north like you said he could. I'd say that made Grover wrong again."

This was a sore point with Harney, who considered himself a better man than Grover, but now he dismissed it with, "Hell, we saved our hides. That's all I figgered on doin'."

"Which way are you riding?" Jedediah asked.

"West," Harney said. "I ain't never ridin' east again. If I

hadn't rode into Hays City goin' east, I never would of got into this mess."

"You keep riding west and you'll wind up in the Pacific," Jedediah said.

"Oh, I'll take a long time gettin' there."

"Why don't you come with me?" Jedediah asked. "You can't go on drifting around forever the way you have. Those days are gone."

"Not for me they ain't," Harney said. "If I stayed in Kansas, I'd have to farm. Mebbe I'd get married and raise me a passel o' kids. No, that ain't no good for me. I'm half alligator, half wolf, and half man, and I got to go where I've got room to howl. I'd ask you to ride with me, but I reckon you've got to see that little gal you left back there."

Jedediah nodded. "That's right. I've got to."

Both were silent for a time, reluctant to hurry the moment of parting and neither knowing what to say now that the time was here. Finally Harney said, "Dunno if it'll work for you or not. It's my guess you've got an itch in your feet the same as I have. But mebbe you'll wind up governor of Kansas." He held out his hand. "So long, Jed."

Jedediah shook hands with him. "So long, Bill."

Without another word Harney mounted and rode west, not bothering to shake hands with anyone else. A strange man, Jedediah told himself, and he wondered if they would have survived if it hadn't been for Harney and his absolute faith that the relief column would come.

After he had said good-bye to Pliley and Stillwell and the rest and had left the fort with Crowell, Jedediah still could not get his mind off Harney. More than any of the others, Jedediah wanted to see him again. Perhaps he would. As Harney had said, you never knew how your stick would float.

"Forsyth's going to make it," Crowell said. "Leastwise, that's what I heard."

Jedediah nodded. "That's what the doctor says, but he'll be a long time getting over it."

"A good man," Crowell said. "I wish I was half as good."

"How do you know you aren't?" Jedediah asked. "I think we all were except Jamey."

"No," Crowell said somberly. "I'm not a good man. That's what makes it hard. I used to think I was. One of the elect, but I found out different."

After that they rode in silence, Crowell lost in the gloom

of his thoughts. He seemed almost as much of a sleepwalker as Matthew Redig. Remembering the old Andy Crowell, Deacon Andy Crowell who had wrapped himself so completely in a cloak of piety, Jedediah decided that the change in him was the strongest of all. Indeed, it was more than a change; it was a rebirth.

Chapter 25

MATTHEW REDIG heard Jedediah call to him as he left the scouts' camp, but he did not look back. He liked Jones better than any other man in the command, but if he had gone back to shake hands, or if he had merely turned and waved, he might have been diverted from what he had to do, and that was a risk he could not take. He had not even bothered to resign. Let them come after him if they wanted to. They wouldn't take him back. Anyhow, he'd be dead long before they found him.

At times his head hurt so much that he could not remember clearly what had happened on the Saline in August. On occasion he had trouble recalling who he was. He often forgot the names of men like Andy Crowell and Jedediah Jones and Sharp Grover, men he had ridden with for days. But it wasn't important. Only one thing was important, and he never forgot it. He must kill Cheyennes.

He rode south slowly, warning himself that he had to be careful not to tire his horse. He might have to look a long time before he found any Cheyennes. When he did glance back an hour later, the tents and the pink stone buildings that made up much of Fort Wallace were lost to sight behind a rise in the prairie.

He went on, each mile taking him deeper into the empty land. He hoped he didn't meet anyone. He was alone now, and that was the way he wanted it. Not that it made any difference whether anyone was with him or not. In reality, he had been alone from the time he had lost Mary and Mark and little Luke.

He had food in his saddlebags but he did not stop for a noon meal. He didn't have much idea where he would find the Cheyennes, but he thought it would be somewhere south of Fort Dodge near the Kansas line. When he got there, he'd just have to hunt until he found them.

That night he camped on a small stream and went on at dawn. Late in the day he crossed the Arkansas. He thought he was a few miles east of Fort Dodge, but he wasn't sure. By sundown the next day he should be in Indian territory. Then he would start the hunt.

The next morning his memory was unusually clear and he thought about what had happened on the island. Some Cheyennes had been killed, but not enough. Not nearly enough. He remembered he had killed five, as many as any of the other scouts unless it was Jack Stillwell or Louis Farley, but he should have killed more. He should have left the island at night and used his knife on some of them. No one had done that except Jones, as far as he knew, and Jones had killed only one.

He tried to remember why he hadn't gone after the Cheyennes at night, but his memory fogged up and he wasn't sure. Maybe it had been because he thought the Indians would attack again, as they had the first day. If they had, he could have stayed in his rifle pit and killed a lot more of them. He had been wrong. They hadn't made another serious attack, so he should have gone after them. Now he must make up for it.

Late in the afternoon he found himself in a broken country of hills and sharp ravines. He topped a crest and looked down upon an Indian village. He wasn't surprised. The only question had been when it would happen. He wasn't sure they were Cheyennes, but that didn't really matter. They were Indians.

He realized instantly that he would be seen if he remained here, silhouetted as he was against the sky, so he rode down the slope, angling toward a brush-choked ravine on his left that ran into the creek in the valley below him.

He pulled up when he reached the ravine and studied the village. Not a large one—a dozen lodges or so. He saw squads moving around and some children playing along the creek, but no braves were in sight. Probably a hunting party had gone out and left the squaws and children here.

Now his memory was as clear and sharp as it had ever been in his life. He remembered leaving his family that day and taking the cow to his neighbor; he remembered returning and seeing the smoke, and finding them, Mary and Mark and baby Luke.

He began to sweat, sick as the memory of it flooded back into his mind. He wiped a hand across his face, thinking that only blood would take the sickness away. A squaw for Mary, two children for Mark and Luke. Drawing his revolver, he checked the loads, then reined up out of the ravine and charged down the grassy slope, his revolver in his right hand.

He was almost in the village before they saw him. He heard them scream as they scurried toward their lodges. He shot one squaw in the back and saw her drop beside her fire. A boy rushed up from the creek and Redig shot him through the heart. He swung his horse toward the stream, and, seeing a tiny girl in the tall grass, he shot her through the head.

He knew there were other children hiding in the grass and willows beside the creek. He dug spurs into his horse's flanks. The animal lunged forward, front hoofs almost trampling a boy who rolled frantically to one side and got up and raced away and fell when Redig fired at him.

He did not see the big boy who ran out of one of the lodges with a bow and arrow. All Redig could think of was that there must be more children hidden here and he had to flush them into the open.

Just as he whirled his horse, the arrow hit him in the chest. He spilled out of his saddle, somehow holding to his revolver, the feathered shaft sticking out of him below his chin. They rushed at him, a horde of screaming women and children. He emptied his gun at them, and then they were on him, slashing and hacking and mutilating.

But Matthew Redig felt nothing. At last he had found the peace he sought.

Chapter 26

Jedediah and Andy Crowell were within sight of Laura's Tit when they saw Jamey Burns standing beside his horse in the road about fifty yards ahead of them.

"What do you know about that?" Jedediah said. "Looks like he's waiting for us. I supposed he was home long before now."

"So did I," Crowell said, "but now that he's here maybe he can't face it."

When they reached the boy, Jedediah saw that he was sullen, his gaze whipping from Jedediah to Crowell and back again. A great many men had reason to be angry at him, Jedediah thought, but Jamey had no right to be angry at anyone.

He said, "Howdy, Jamey," and pulled up, realizing that the boy would not look at himself as others did. He'd had plenty of time to think up excuses for himself during the long ride from Fort Wallace.

Crowell said, "We thought you'd be home before now, Jamey."

"I've been waiting for you." Jamey motioned toward a clump of trees to his left. "I camped there waiting for you. You've been a long time coming."

"If you're mad because you had to wait for us, you can get out of the way," Jedediah said. "Nobody asked you to wait. And another thing: you've got no call to blame anyone else for what you did."

"I'm not," Jamey said quickly. "It's just that I couldn't go home till I had seen you. I've been waiting for three days and I thought I had missed you."

"What's so important about seeing us?" Crowell asked. "You're close to home. Why didn't you go on?"

"I got this close and then I couldn't go any farther," Jamey blurted out. "There's something I had to know. Are you going to tell about me?"

Jedediah understood then. The boy would not go home if he knew he would see contempt in people's eyes. He had been able to stand it on the island and during the march south to Fort Wallace, but he could not face it for a lifetime if he saw it in the eyes of his parents and his neighbors—Ruth Tilton most of all.

Jedediah glanced at Crowell, then he said, "Jamey, what you tell folks is your business. I don't consider it my duty to tell anyone anything, but fooling other people won't be enough. You can't fool yourself. Not for long anyhow."

"I'll take care of that," Jamey said shrilly. "I just want to know if you're going to tattle on me."

"No," Jedediah said.

"I won't, either," Crowell said, "but it's like Slim says. You won't . . ."

Jamey mounted and, turning his horse, put the animal

into a gallop. Jedediah watched him for a moment, then shook his head. "Andy, that boy is dead. What he did on the island will eat his insides out."

Crowell nodded. "I wish we could do something for him, but I don't think anyone can."

"I don't think so, either," Jedediah said. They went on, Jedediah adding thoughtfully, "It's like the salvation you used to talk about. Talking about it and being baptized aren't enough. Seems to me that something has to happen inside a man."

"I know it now," Crowell said. "I didn't know it before I left." He chewed on his lower lip a moment, then he changed the subject. "I reckon you'll be seeing Cally."

"First thing," Jedediah said. "If she hasn't waited for me, I guess I'd be about as bad off as Jamey. I couldn't blame her if she hasn't. I didn't give her any reason to wait."

"We've all made our mistakes," Crowell said, "and we can be thankful the Lord let us live to make up for 'em."

They rode in silence after that, as they had most of the way from Fort Wallace. When they reached the lane that led to Crowell's farm, he reined up and held out his hand. "So long, Slim," he said. "Stop by if you take a notion to leave the country."

Jedediah shook hands with him. "Maybe I won't leave for a while. All depends on Cally."

"Good luck," Crowell said. "I wish I was in your shoes. I'd have it easier than I will trying to explain things to Sadie."

He nodded and turned up the lane. The farm looked the same as when he left. Not that he expected any change. Sadie would look after things as well as he could, better than he had in the past. He reined up at the kitchen door and dismounted wearily, hating the prospect of listening to his wife's strident voice as she condemned him for leaving her. Even more than that, he hated to humble himself as he knew he must.

He opened the back door and went in. Sadie was standing at the stove frying a chicken. Her back was to him, but he was quite sure she had seen him riding in from the road. If she hadn't, she would have turned around to see who had come in.

"I'm back, Sadie," he said.

"Sure, and ain't you the hero," she said. "Everybody's been talking about it ever since we heard what happened. I seen the Burns kid ride by while ago, so I knew you'd be along. Well, I killed a rooster, knowing you'd figure you had to have a big dinner when you got home, being a hero and all."

He stood just inside the door, anger growing in him as he stared at her broad, unyielding back. He was tempted to get on his horse and keep on riding, but he couldn't. Not yet anyhow. Not until he had tried to live with her. He had changed, and he hoped that in time she would too.

"Charley Higgins was over this morning," she went on. "Folks are planning a big shindig to honor you heroes. Charley, he said to let him know as soon as you got here. They hadn't heard a good sermon since you left. They'll want you to preach tonight. Time they was hearing the Word the way it ought to be spoke, he said."

"They won't hear it from me. I ain't worthy to preach it." He strode to the stove and, taking her by the shoulder, turned her around to face him. "I've been wrong. I guess that's what you wanted to hear and you're sure going to hear it."

He swallowed, staring at her stony face; then he made himself go on. "I used to believe God talked to me. Me, Andy Crowell, who was a little better'n anybody else because of it and because I could preach and tell Charley Higgins and the Tiltons and the rest of 'em they was saved. That was what they wanted to hear. Made 'em feel better'n their neighbors. Well, I ain't going to tell 'em that no more. I'm going to quit gadding around and I'll stay here and do the farming like a man should. I'm no hero, neither. You might as well know it right now."

She had been hurt by him and she wanted to hurt him back, but now most of her reason for wanting to hurt him was gone. She was plainly bewildered, never expecting to hear this kind of talk from him. She stood there staring at him, not knowing what to do or say.

Finally she asked in a small voice, "You mean that, Andy?"

"I mean it," he said. "When I was on the island I found out I wasn't talking to God. I was too scared when the Indians were coming at us. And another thing. I found out I didn't believe as much in going to Heaven as I thought I did. That first morning when it looked like the Indians were going to wipe us out, the Colonel asked for someone to pray, but I couldn't. It was the first I ever had a chance to pray and couldn't do it. Afterwards when it looked like we would starve to death, I prayed for myself. Not anyone else on the island. Just myself. Seemed like I didn't really care about the others. Then I took a good look at myself and I was ashamed. Right then I knew I wasn't saved."

He stopped, sick with self-condemnation as the memory of those hopeless days on the island rushed into his consciousness. He plunged on as if he had to get this said. "I talked to the men about salvation while we was marching, but they wouldn't listen. Then when they would have listened I couldn't talk about it. I knew God hadn't been talking to me like I'd bragged about Him doing, but He talked to me then, all right. He said, 'Andy, you've been going around telling folks a lot of things that ain't true, like being saved, but you've been dead wrong. You've got to work on it all your life and you ain't been working very hard. All you've been doing is talk.' Well Sadie, I aim to start working on it right here."

She kept on staring at him, wide-eyed, as if she couldn't believe she was actually hearing him say these things. Suddenly she began to cry and turned back to the stove. "I'm sorry about the things I said, Andy. I was so mad when you left that I said I hoped they scalped you, but I didn't mean it. I didn't mean it at all, Andy."

"I guess you had a right to be mad," he said.

Remembering that he hadn't kissed her the morning he left, he put an arm around her and hugged her, then he kissed her on the cheek. He knew it wouldn't always be like this. She'd find plenty of excuses to rawhide him with her tongue, but at least he could fix it so she'd have to hunt to find an excuse.

"Andy!" Her leathery face turned red. "You go sit down at the table. I'll have your supper ready in a minute."

He obeyed, smiling a little. Now that he had got it all said, he felt better. The future wouldn't be so bad. He'd see to that. At least he was sure he had learned one thing on the island. If he was going to save his soul, this was the place to start.

Chapter 27

JAMEY BURNS rode slowly after he passed Andy Crowell's lane. He remembered how many times when he was huddling in his rifle pit that he had wished he was here. If he ever got back, he would never resent hoeing corn or doing anything else his father wanted him to.

He remembered how it had been the night it rained and he was shivering in his trench and wondering if Indians were crawling all over the island and would be jumping down on him with knives in their hands. He'd thought about his own bed and how good it would be to lie in it again.

Later, when he was starving, with nothing to eat except rotten horse meat that smelled and tasted so bad that he often threw it up after he had eaten it, he'd thought about the meals he'd had at home, the special dishes his mother cooked for him because he liked them. He even dreamed about sitting at the table and reaching for a piece of custard pie, but he always woke just before his hand touched the food, the smell of putrid flesh poisoning his nostrils.

Ever since he had left Fort Wallace, he had been telling himself it would be good to be back, to do the work he used to try to get out of doing and to sleep in his own bed and sit at the table and eat and eat until his stomach was full again. But now he was here and it didn't feel good at all.

His mother would make over him and maybe he could sneak off and see Ruth Tilton. The trouble was, old man Tilton would be after him with a shotgun. And that wouldn't be the worst. His Pa would cuss him out for leaving with the fall work coming on, and if he happened to be drunk just when Jamey got back, he might try to take the strap to him. No, that wasn't the worst, either. He could stand things like that. The one thing he couldn't stand was for them to find out about him.

And Ruth? Those crazy stories he had told her about riding a white horse and having a sword and telling Sheridan what to do! He was going to capture Dull Knife and Black Kettle and Roman Nose. Yes, even Roman Nose.

Suddenly the tears began rolling down his cheeks. After

all his dreams and the bragging he had done to Ruth, he was back with nothing except the bitter memory of his cowardice. He hadn't even seen Roman Nose, because he'd been cowering in his rifle pit, but he knew from the talk how close it had been, how near the Indians had come to overrunning the island and killing all of them. It would have been better for him if they had killed him.

He couldn't face Ruth and have her look at him as if she was sure he had done all the fine things he'd said he was going to. Oh, he could lie to her and she would believe it for a while. But someday she'd find out. Everybody would find out. Even his mother would know. He couldn't face that. He just couldn't.

At that moment he didn't even want to live. He wished he'd got up out of his rifle pit and fought with the rest of the scouts. He'd wished that a thousand times. But his life had been made up of wishes and dreams. Poor stuff. He was no part of a man. Mr. Jones had told him he had to live with himself. Now he knew what the teacher had meant, knew that the shame in him would never go away.

He was in front of the house before he realized it. He started to turn the horse. He could not face his folks or Ruth or anyone else. He would have ridden away if his mother had not come out of the chicken house at that moment.

She screamed, "Link, Jamey's home!" and ran to him.

He couldn't leave now. Maybe he could later, after he'd had a meal and told them some lies about how brave he'd been. He wasn't sure of anything except that he couldn't stay. He dismounted and, dropping the reins, turned toward his mother.

He hugged her and held her while she cried, then she kissed him. "I knew you'd be back, Jamey," she whispered. "I never really prayed for anything in my life before, but I prayed for you to be saved, and I knew the good Lord would answer my prayer." She drew back to look at him, her hands coming up to touch his face. "You're so thin, Jamey. I should have known you would be, starving for so long on that island. I'll cook you anything you want. We'll get the pounds back on you."

His father was there then, slapping him on the back and bellowing, "By God, son, we're proud of you! I didn't think you had it in you. We've heard the whole story, how you boys fought off a thousand Injuns and almost starved to death before they found you. It was something you won't never forget, wasn't it?"

"No." Jamey swallowed. "No, I sure won't."

"We're going to have some big doings around here, I can tell you," Link Burns went on, still shouting his words. "Purty damned good to have three Laura's Tit men in that fight. We're going to celebrate it. We've been talking about it ever since we heard. Me'n Higgins and Tilton and a lot of folks. Next Sunday, I reckon it'll be, with Deacon Crowell preaching the Word, and a big dinner, with you and the Deacon and the school teacher telling us about it."

"Pa, he's hungry and tired," Mrs. Burns said. "I'll get supper started and you go over and tell the Tiltons. Ruth will be right over. Maybe her Pa and Ma will come too. Jamey, you come into the house and tell me all about it while I cook supper."

"I'll ride your horse over to the Tiltons," Link said. "Save me saddling up." He looked the horse over critically, then shrugged. "Well, I guess you didn't lose nothing on the swap."

Jamey went into the house with his mother, thinking that during the days he'd been on the island he had never thought this moment would come. Now he wished it hadn't. He wished he was back on the island. Anywhere but here.

He'd lie to them. He'd have to. But sooner or later Mr. Jones or Andy Crowell would let the truth slip, even if neither one intended to. Or maybe McCall or Pliley or some-one else who had been on the island would ride through and hear this was his home and the story would come out.

He stood in the kitchen while his mother beat up some eggs for a custard pie, all the time rattling on about how proud everybody was of him and how much they had missed him. "It's kind of queer the way it's worked out," she said. "You know we never liked the Tiltons and they sure didn't like us, but after you left, Ruth came over and we got ac-quainted. She's a nice girl, Jamey, and she loves you so much. After her Pa found out where you'd gone, he changed too. He's willing for you and Ruth to get married. Link and me have talked it over with them. You can stay right here with us and Ruth can help me with the housework. And another thing that's queer is the way your Pa has quit drinking and been working hard. Of course he's had to, with you gone and all, but it's more'n that, Jamey. He even went to church once with the Tiltons and he's been looking forward to next

Sunday like he said, a big dinner in the church and the celebration."

Jamey was hearing the words, but they were words without meaning. He stood at the window staring across the prairie toward the Tilton place. He gripped the casing, his muscles turning to rubber. He saw Ruth running toward him, her hair flying behind her. He choked and tried to say something, but no words came out. His head was about to explode. He couldn't stand it, Ruth looking at him and trusting him and believing the lies he would have to tell her.

He whirled away from the window and stumbled out of the room. His mother called, "Jamey, what is it?"

He said something about going to his room. He couldn't stand it. He couldn't even stand himself. He should have died back there on that damned island. But he hadn't. Now death was the only escape.

His mother heard his door slam. She started after him, and stopped, thinking she had better let him alone. No one knew what he had been through. They would have to be kind and understanding and give him time to get used to the dull life at home. Ruth would help him. They were both pretty young, but . . .

She heard the report of the gun. She screamed, knowing belatedly that she should have followed him.

She rushed into his room and found him lying on the floor, his gun beside him. He had shot himself through the head.

Chapter 28

JEDEDIAH saw Cally standing in front of her house when he was still a long way off, shading her eyes with a hand as she stared against the slanting sunlight. She could not have known he was back, he thought. Had she stood there every day watching for him, from the time she had heard about the battle and that he was alive? But maybe she was looking for someone else, and not for him at all. Maybe she had married a farmer who wanted a housekeeper, a woman to keep him warm at night. Or maybe she was promised.

These were the things he had been afraid would happen. He could not blame her if they were true; he could not blame her for anything she had done. He had no claim upon her. He hadn't even written to her after he had returned to Fort Wallace. But now that he was this close, anxiety pushed at him; he had to know. He spurred his tired horse to a faster pace. Still she stood there, motionless, long after he was close enough for her to recognize him.

When he reached her and dismounted, he stood as frozen as she was, unable to cross the short space between them, afraid to know the truth. He had expected her to come bouncing to him as she used to, filled with vitality and love for him and all of life, but now she could only say in a neutral voice, "How are you, Jedediah?"

He might have been away for weeks on a job of some kind, just an ordinary job working cattle or shucking corn or teaching school. But what else could he expect after the way he had treated her? She had every right to hate him. If this short space of less than ten feet was to be crossed, he would have to do it; he had to humble himself just as Andy Crowell must do before his wife, and in a way it was as hard as anything he had done on the island.

He walked to her slowly. He said, "I'm back, Cally. I'm back because I learned something while I was gone. I'm back because I love you and want to marry you."

Still she stood there as if she didn't hear. She said, "You're so thin, Jedediah."

"Cally, I've been wrong." He took her hands, his big, bony-knuckled ones holding hers as if he would never let her go. "John Donne was right when he said, 'No man is an island, entire of itself.' You were right in quoting him. I was wrong. I thought I could live without being involved with anyone or anything, but it didn't take me long to learn that my life depended on the others, and their lives depended upon me."

He wasn't getting through to her, and for a horrible moment he thought he never would. Suddenly the things that had been so important to him when he was on the island—a decent meal and a warm bed and a breath of sweet, pure air, even life itself—were not as important as making her understand, bringing her back to him as she had been the night he had left her.

"I'm asking you to forgive me, Cally," he said. "You knew me better than I knew myself. You said I must have been terribly hurt. You were right. I loved my father very much, but when I was a boy he ran off with a woman and left me. I never saw him again. After that I was afraid to love anyone or let anyone love me. I never really understood that until we were way out there by ourselves chasing a bunch of Indians that was maybe twenty times as big as we were. I didn't think any of us would live through it. When you get to feeling that way, you sort things out in your mind and you know what's real and what isn't. I knew there was no illusion about love, and that you were right when you said the only way to be happy is to be involved with the people you love. I know I was a coward when I ran away from you that night. I was afraid of love, but I'm not now."

Then, because he could not stand it any longer, he put his arms around her and brought her hard against him and kissed her, and suddenly she came alive, her lips sweet and eager upon his. When she drew back, she looked at him, smiling. She said softly, "I thought you were never coming back. I thought I had lost you."

"Then you'll marry me?"

"Tonight," she answered. "Tomorrow. Next week. Any time you say."

"Oh, Cally, Cally, I was afraid . . ."

He stopped, remembering there was something else he had to tell her that might make a difference. "Cally, I can't stay here all my life. Maybe I've got itchy feet, but that isn't all of it. I got to thinking while we were on the island that it was strange I was allowed to live when others died, and it seemed to me there was no answer. I hadn't done what I was brought into the world to do, so I had to live a little longer. I don't know what it is, but I've got to go hunting for it. If you marry me, I'll take you to places where you'll be cold and hungry and maybe in danger. It's something I can't help. If you—"

She put a hand over his lips. She smiled as she said, " 'Intreat me not to leave thee, or to return from following after thee: for whither thou goest, I will go, and where thou lodgest, I will lodge.' Ruth said that to her mother-in-law, but I'm saying it to the man I love. I've never asked for an easy life, Jedediah."

He was kissing her again when her mother called from the house, "Supper's ready, Cally. Bring him in and feed him. Pa will take care of his horse."

She took his hand and led him toward the house, saying, "We heard some of the things that happened, but we'll want to hear all about it from you. It must have been terrible."

He was thinking of her mother's words, "Supper's ready,"

words he never expected to hear again. When he thought about what had happened, the worst was not the Indians, but the gnawing hunger, the sickening stench, eating the stinking horse meat. But Cally would never understand how it had been. No one could who had not been there.

"It was pretty bad," he said, and let it go at that.

Wayne D. Overholser has won three Golden Spur awards from the Western Writers of America and has a long list of fine Western titles to his credit. He was born in Pomeroy, Washington, and attended the University of Montana, University of Oregon, and the University of Southern California before becoming a public school teacher and principal in various Oregon communities. He began writing for Western pulp magazines in 1936 and within a couple of years was a regular contributor to Street & Smith's *Western Story* and Fiction House's *Lariat Story Magazine. Buckaroo's Code* (1948) was his first Western novel and remains one of his best. In the 1950s and 1960s, having retired from academic work to concentrate on writing, he would publish as many as four books a year under his own name or a pseudonym, most prominently as Joseph Wayne. *The Bitter Night, The Lone Deputy,* and *The Violent Land* are among the finest of the early Overholser titles. He was asked by William MacLeod Raine, that dean among Western writers, to complete his last novel after Raine's death. Some of Overholser's most rewarding novels were actually collaborations with other Western writers: *Colorado Gold* with Chad Merriman and *Showdown at Stony Creek* with Lewis B. Patten. Overholser's Western novels, no matter under what name they have been published, are based on a solid knowledge of the history and customs of the American frontier West, particularly when set in his two favorite Western states, Oregon and Colorado. When it comes to his characters, he writes with skill, an uncommon sensitivity, and a consistently vivid and accurate vision of a way of life unique in human history.